SNOW CANDY

**OTHER BOOKS BY TERRY CARROLL**
*Body Contact* (A Carl North Mystery)
*No Blood Relative*

# SNOW CANDY

### A CARL NORTH MYSTERY

## BY TERRY CARROLL

THE MERCURY PRESS

The publisher gratefully acknowledges the financial assistance of the Canada Council for the Arts, the Ontario Arts Council, and the Ontario Book Publishing Tax Credit Program. The publisher further acknowledges the financial support of the Government of Canada through the Department of Canadian Heritage's Book Publishing Industry Development Program (BPIDP) for our publishing activities.

Editor: Beverley Daurio
Cover, composition and page design: Beverley Daurio


Printed and bound in Canada
Printed on acid-free paper

1 2 3 4 5    11 10 09 08 07

Library and Archives Canada Cataloguing in Publication
Carroll, Terry
Snow candy : a Carl North mystery / Terry Carroll.
ISBN 1-55128-135-X
I. Title.
PS8555.A7717S64 2007        C813'.54        C2007-907457-X


The Mercury Press
Box 672, Station P, Toronto, Ontario  Canada  M5S 2Y4
www.themercurypress.ca

In memory of my father, Harold M. Carroll, 1921 – 2007

## PROLOGUE

A raucous whining drew Hughie Campbell from a dream. With his right hand, Hughie rubbed his left cheek. His heavy sweater smelled of oil and mould. The kitchen was cooling. Light and shadows danced around the walls, the floor, the table. That was strange. Why would his mother bring out the coal oil lamp?

He lifted his head and attempted to raise himself. On the second try, with the help of quivering hands, he made it. He shuffled to the window. Rain had started in the morning, had begun to freeze around noon. The power had been knocked out mid-afternoon. It was now night, but outside was more white than black. He wiped at a frosted window pane with one bare palm, melting a hole in the ice. Over by the silo, two snowmobiles idled. Snow streaked in wraiths across their headlights.

Two of the buggers.

Trespassing.

Horse thieves, maybe.

A good team like Charlie and Barney would fetch as much as six hundred apiece, more for stud. Hughie's dad loved horses, and Hughie hated men who tampered with them. "Good for nuffin," he said out loud.

He steadied himself and paused, before making his way to the wood stove that was still warm to the touch. Neighbours said he was soft in the head, keeping that stove when he also had the electric. With no heat, what would those geniuses be saying tonight? He had to force his left leg. It had stiffened up as he slept in the chair. He should have gone to bed. But then he wouldn't have spotted the snowmobiles.

The rifle behind the old stove was loaded. He thought it was. He was pretty sure. If it wasn't, the threat of it might do the trick. Hughie tucked the .22 under his good arm and made his way back across the green linoleum, ripped to black patches in places. With his thin right shoulder, he bumped the outside door. Nothing. He hit it again. Harder, hurting something inside. The ice seal along the edges crackled, and the door swung wide.

Wind and cold surged around him in sharp waves. He leaned against the frame. His dad's voice came to him, moist and soft, a rivulet of tobacco juice trickling a line from his mouth to his stubbly chin. "What do you expect, Hughie? It's January."

Hughie raised his left arm as high as it would go, somewhere around his waist. He sent his stiffening trigger hand even lower, to aim above the intruders. That was the idea. His body carried remnants of instincts for such things, ancient senses of line and angle.

Those men had no right. This was a Campbell farm and the Campbells...

As if it had a life of its own, the rifle fired.

A headlight shattered.

The figures turned toward the house. Hughie cursed them; what were they, Eskimos? Out on a night like this, robbing old bachelors minding their own business? He heard them shout, couldn't make out what they were saying. They let go of something they'd been dragging toward the silo and waddled to their snowmobiles.

Take that, you buggers.

The figures started their machines but didn't skedaddle. They roared toward the house. The one with no headlight followed in a line behind the other. Hughie watched this longer than was sensible before he closed the door and hobbled to one of his round-backed kitchen chairs. The rifle, he laid on the table in front of him, handy in the light of the lamp. He rubbed his numb left arm with his right.

Light flared through the ice-encrusted kitchen window.

The engines idled and stopped.

Steps thumped up the stairs to the side porch.

The door flung open.

Two men entered, closing the wind behind them. Hughie raised the rifle with his good hand. He had never fully recovered from the stroke, but he wasn't an idiot. The angle was wrong.

The bigger man, massive in his parka, glanced at the gun and snarled, "You stupid old geezer. What you gonna do with a single-shot .22? Ever hear the term, reload?"

His shorter companion's laugh was high-pitched. He had a red beard flecked with grey. Hughie thought he recognized the laughing man. But no name would come to him. Hughie wanted to tell them to get out. His toothless mouth rummaged around. The words, in there somewhere, would not surface.

The large man raised his right hand and set his own gun on the table. With careful deliberation, he removed bulky mitts one at a time and picked up his weapon again. He pointed it at Hughie.

What an asshole, Hughie thought. Any fool knows guns like that are illegal. He'd seen it on the CBC.

The red-haired man said, "Do we have to, Turk?"

The man who said that… what was it about him? He put Hughie in mind of a woman, but who?

"We don't need no witnesses. Look at this pigsty. Let's do the world a favour."

A tattoo of a snake's head, its tongue flicking, ended near the man's thumb. That digit settled on the guard. The index finger next to it curled comfortably around the trigger. Hughie raised his working arm in protest, .22 at the ready.

## CHAPTER 1

Firefighters had set up powerful klieg lights on snowbanks and the running boards of trucks. The lights illuminated the remains of a farmhouse, stark against the wintry backdrop. Thick icicles and thinner sheets of ice glistered from the burned remnants of walls and a collapsed roof. One pumper truck was still spraying water. Figures came and went.

It was after 5:00 a.m. On New Year's Eve, the temperature had started to drop. Before midnight, a minor blizzard had hurled in off Lake Erie. Sergeant Carl North inhaled through his nose, broken in a hockey accident and never properly straightened. He held that breath all the way to his abdomen, before exhaling through his mouth, and holding again before the next inhalation. He repeated this. Much as he hated winter, he was glad the air was cold and fresh.

His queasiness settled, North forced his attention back to the scene inside the kitchen. Warmth seeped up through his boots and into his feet. Constable Pete Heemstra stood beside him on the concrete step. Below them, Constable Jennifer Duchamps stamped her feet on snow-swept ground. Jennifer and Pete were plain clothes officers, reporting to North in Criminal Investigations in St. Thomas.

Crispy critters. Sergeant Carl North thought the two bodies looked like crispy critters. He forced his gaze away from the remains. Holes had burned through the farmhouse flooring in places, exposing the tops of charred joists. What was left of the linoleum, what wasn't completely fried, curled at the edges. Old appliances, laden with blackened debris, tilted against the far wall. The scene smelled of soot and charcoal and decay. And an underlying stench like burned meat.

The bodies were lying about three feet apart on the kitchen floor. They looked like dead fighters, as if two boxers had been biblically slain, mid-swing, by fire and brimstone. But North had seen this before, in a fire in the Belleford area. Extreme heat caused muscles to contract after death. Arms and legs flexed at the joints, creating a pugilistic effect.

The position also put North in mind of Connie, sleeping, the way she drew her legs up and wrapped her arms around a pillow. The image was morbid, and he shoved it away. He needed to be a good observer and analyzer, as unemotional as possible.

North tried to speak and failed. He cleared his throat and started again. "Won't be much in the way of fingerprints." Heat had seared the flesh off fingers and toes, enhancing the zombie effect.

One figure was taller. Its clothing and flesh, where flesh remained, had melded together. Its torso had apparently shrunk in the fire.

The other figure was shorter, and its clothing and flesh had burned more evenly. Skeletal remains of feet poked through burned leather footwear.

North concentrated his flashlight on the upper body of this figure. The smaller dead man had skull damage, possibly caused by falling debris or extreme heat. The burned rifle near him suggested something else.

Pete seemed to pick up on North's train of thought. "Looks like somebody used a weapon a lot bigger than that squirrel gun." The beam of Pete's flashlight indicated the rifle at an angle about a meter from the bodies. "A .22 would make a pinhole by comparison."

North said, "In Nunavut, I met this guy in a bar. Claimed he'd been shot in the head with a .22 by his brother. He carried the bullet in his skull. He was one lucky asshole."

"Or one of the world's great liars." Jennifer said.

North swung the light toward her and then down to the right below the step. He circled it around snow drifts between the house and a silo. "That sure looks like a snowmobile track. You can see it between drifts. It took a swing over there." He passed the beam of the light in a sweeping arc to the left and back to the right. "Looks like it stopped near the house. We may be able to get a decent footprint or two. Did we call Forensics?"

"Not easy to find people New Year's Eve," Jennifer said. "They'd rather leave it to Scenes of Crime officers. Let me check on their progress." She removed her gloves and used her cell phone to call the station.

Pete said, "With all this traffic, we'll have trouble proving much."

"What was a snowmobile doing here? And a track that's been driven over means somebody was here before emergency service vehicles."

Pete said, "Good point."

"We need to tape off the area where you can see tracks and also here, where somebody got off. I want pictures of tracks and foot imprints. We'll ask Forensics and the uniformed Ident officer to get us a cast of any usable footprint."

"Can't be easy in snow."

"Don't you remember any of this from police college in Aylmer? Everything depends on the type of snow and the temperature. To get a decent photo, they may want to spraypaint the footprint or even apply snow print wax."

"Do we have snow print wax?"

North swivelled toward Jennifer, who had ended her call. "Let's find out. Jennifer, what did dispatch say about Forensics?"

"They located somebody. Might even be sober."

"Okay, call them back and make sure they bring a footprint kit. We need wax and the heated sulphur stuff plus dental stone. If we don't have a kit, ask them to contact the OPP." North exhaled a stream of vapour as he added, "Don't forget, we want photos before they try a cast in the snow."

Jennifer offered a mock salute, grinned and said, "Aye, aye, Sir."

"Next time I'm up this late I hope to have a drink in one hand and a blond in the other." North pushed the stem of his watch and glanced at its green face. He stepped down to ground level. "It's almost 5:30. We've got a lot to do, and we need the help of our brothers and sisters in fire investigation. Has anybody contacted the coroner?"

"We called," Jennifer said. "Want to run a pool on how fast he'll come on a night like this?"

North left Pete and Jennifer to secure the scene with caution tape. He headed toward a group of police and fire officers huddled together, shoulders hunched, feet stomping to generate heat. Except for trees rattling when the wind blew and one lone, phallic silo, the burned house was all that remained in the farmyard. The barns had collapsed on their foundations some time ago. A silver moon was obscured and revealed and hidden again by white slips of clouds.

An enormous hairy cat rubbed North's leg and yowled. He stumbled, slipped on an icy patch and went down, banging his left knee. The pain was instant and tooth-ache sharp.

From where he sprawled, he kicked in the direction of the cat. "Get outta here."

Constable Pete Heemstra laughed and called, "Where's your skates, Gumper?" The nickname, based on North's amateur goaltending and the legendary NHL goalie Gump Worsley, had started when he and Pete had been stationed together in Belleford. The Belleford police had so badly wanted to rid themselves of North, they'd given him a glowing recommendation the previous year, when he'd applied for a transfer to St. Thomas and the job as sergeant. After he'd nabbed the job, he'd convinced Pete Heemstra to follow him.

"In my hockey bag. Where your head'll be if you don't keep your mouth shut." North rolled to his feet. He tried his leg. The knee accepted the weight. What did North hate most about winter: the cold, the dark, or the ice? Close call, but he probably found the darkness the most depressing.

Pete sounded cheerful, a good-time guy at heart. "You hear about the two drunks from North Bay?"

North hop-stepped forward, loose-jointed, like a man with one shoe untied. As he did this, the pain diminished. A good sign. "Don't think I did."

Pete turned to Constable Jennifer Duchamps. "These two young guys, see, they been at the bar for hours. They decide to go ice fishing. Just as they're about to fire up the auger, this booming voice says, 'There are no fish here.'

"'Yeah, right,' says one of the guys.

"They stagger around, trying to manhandle the auger when they hear the same huge voice. 'There are no fish here.'

"One of the drunks gets a little scared, and he says, 'Who is this? God?'

"'No,' the voice said. 'And the rink's closed.'"

Firefighters and police officers chuckled. The most North managed was a smile under his trimmed moustache. Cold was creeping inside his parka and down his neck. He shivered and hoped nobody noticed. He buttoned his coat to his neck.

A pumper truck shunted backward and forward, moving out of a rut as it prepared to leave. North joined Pete and a fire investigator, Henry Shaw, a slim man with a deeply lined face who had cancer. He looked like a ghost of his former self. North's breath swirled like cigarette smoke. "Happy New Year, Henry. Two fires in one night. No euchre for the overnight shift."

"The one at Saint Tease in town looked like natural gas. Not sure what's going on with this one."

North stamped his feet—he could still feel his knee—and rubbed his arms. "My crew didn't get called to the strip club fire."

"Constable Skelding was looking after things. Hard to tell with natural gas fires, but no injuries or deaths, nothing suspicious. Not yet, anyway."

North ran his gloved hand over the ridge in his nose. "According to dispatch, this 911 address is where one Hugh Campbell called home."

Out of nowhere—it must have been that word 'home'—Connie's voice flashed through his mind. "You got to stay warm, sweets." Sometimes she said "gots." There seemed to be no good way to tell people about the break-up. North's first marriage had gone down the drain and the second one was almost there.

A female uniformed officer—North came up blank when he tried to recall her name—said, "We assume one of the deceased is Mr. Campbell."

For a millisecond, North wondered what she was talking about. He shook his head and reached inside his parka for the stubby notepad in his shirt pocket. Letting in the cold again. He said to nobody in particular, "So what do you think? Husband and wife? An old place like this goes up like a tinderbox. What chance do a couple of old farts have? A few minutes and they're overcome by smoke."

Jennifer had joined the circle. Jennifer started to answer, but Pete Heemstra talked over her. She looked frustrated and turned away as Pete said, "We're almost positive we're looking at two men."

"So two brothers, a couple of old bachelors?"

"Or two guys in a gay marriage, like a domestic? One guy shoots the other and turns a gun on himself?"

North replaced the notepad in his pocket. He shot Pete a sceptical look. "Anything's possible. I want everybody to stay open-minded." He surveyed the destroyed farmhouse. "We got the call instead of the OPP. So this is part of St. Thomas, eh?"

Jennifer said, "We're a kilometre west and another kilometre north of the city proper. But after annexation, we're standing in St. Thomas."

"Guess that's how we preserve farmland for future generations."

Jennifer laughed, clapped her gloves together for warmth and stamped her feet. "C'mon, this will make a lovely subdivision one of these days."

North turned to Henry Shaw and asked him if he had anything to add.

"Even with the other fire," Henry Shaw said as the three men, followed by Constable Duchamps, moved back toward the house, "we were here inside 15 or 20 minutes. A neighbour happened to be up for a whiz or something and called it in."

Henry turned toward the road where a ditched fire truck sat crossways, its front lights tilted down. "Too bad the new guy thinks he's a NASCAR driver."

North said, "We all learn about winter driving the hard way."

"You asked about evidence, Sarge." Pete said to North. "There's only a crawl space under the kitchen, no basement. We should be checking for incendiary devices in the kitchen."

"We need to keep out the lovely white stuff, as much as we can," North said. "You boys have a big tarp?"

Henry nodded.

"And you'll loan it to your fellow municipal employees?"

"Course you can borrow it." Henry gobbed spittle into the snow. "And we'll both need the lights. A couple of us will be here for a while. We'll keep the one truck and the light source, unless we get another call. Not sure we could handle a hat trick."

"Okay. Pierre, you and Constable Duchamps and a couple of the uniforms do your best to tarp the kitchen like a circus tent. Make sure the elephants and the monkeys do the least possible damage to the scene. I'll get dispatch to call the coroner again."

Flashing lights rotated from the side road. A heavy tow vehicle was backing toward the ditched fire truck. "Deano's here," Henry said.

"Should we also request an ambulance?" Jennifer asked.

"Not yet." North wiped wet snow from his face and sucked on a false front tooth, the upshot of an old meeting with a hockey stick. "Get me everything you can before they haul the bodies away. Let's secure a wide area. Thanks for the lights, Henry. They'll be a big help."

"One thing before we start." Pete coughed into a black leather glove and turned to Henry Shaw. "Do you see any connection between the two fires?"

Henry's angular face showed interest. "You mean, tonight, like? We'll need a formal investigation to determine the causes."

"I know that. But just between us kittens, you didn't notice any similarities?"

"A strip joint and a farm. Nothing to connect them that I can see."

North probed a little. "What's tickling that feeble mind of yours, Pierre?"

Pete shook his head and brushed snow and loose bits of soot off his pant legs. "We'll take nothing but pictures and leave nothing but footprints. Don't tell Sergeant North I said that."

North persisted. "You noticed something."

"The way those bodies are lying. I don't know, like somebody placed them there. I'm also curious whether the .22 was fired."

## CHAPTER 2

An itch, a longing, crept up North's arms and invaded his throat, his mouth. He sucked on his false front tooth, drew it in a little and set it back in place with his tongue. Pete approached his unmarked Crown Vic. North was already in the driver's seat, Jennifer in the back. No hint of dawn yet. Uniformed officers appeared and disappeared, stepping in and out of the light.

As soon as Pete had ducked into the front passenger seat, North asked, "Can I bum a smoke?"

"Criminal Investigations getting to you?"

North's voice rose a notch. "A cigarette. Not your first-born."

Pete reached into his shirt pocket. "You may want to consider heroin. Cheaper and easier to quit."

Pete flipped him a duMaurier and leaned over to light it. From the middle of the back seat, Jennifer said, "You two addicts mind opening a window, let a girl who cares about her body get a little air?"

Pete and North pushed power window buttons almost simultaneously. Pete said, "With a body like yours, *somebody* should be taking care of it."

Jennifer slapped the back of Pete's head.

North inhaled. Nicotine surged through him like electricity through a barbed wire fence. "The last thing I need is a highly sexualized atmosphere. I just took the course, and it's my legal responsibility to inform you of that."

Jennifer chuckled. "What's the world coming to? You moon the wrong person at the office Christmas party, and suddenly you're not 'professional' any more."

"I try to do the right thing by feminism in the twenty-first century. I really do." North was laughing as he extracted the stubby notepad and pen from his shirt pocket. "Anything new from the scene?'

Pete pulled a clear plastic bag out of his coat pocket. "One .22 shell. So the rifle was fired. Don't worry, I used gloves when I picked it up."

"Nothing heavier?"

"That's the only casing we found. You probably think you'd find more if you went over the area yourself. But I'm telling you, you wouldn't."

"So nothing of a larger calibre." North drew deeply on his cigarette. His fingers trembled. "Maybe the shooter cleaned up after himself. What about you, Jen-Jen? You see anything?"

"I'm sure one of the deceased *is* Hughie Campbell." Constable Jennifer Duchamps leaned forward from the back seat. "The smaller man, the one who appears to have been shot."

North noted the use of "Hughie." "You are acquainted with the owner of this property?"

"He must be about a hundred years old. No, I'm exaggerating, but he'd be in his eighties. A real old bachelor farmer—information I was trying to convey to you gentlemen earlier, but nobody was prepared to listen."

"And you know this, how?"

"He went to Cowal United Church, where I went as a kid. I was a McKillop, don't you know? Raised about ten miles west of the city, in the heart of Cowal. It would have been closer for Hughie to attend church in St. Thomas, but he stayed loyal to the old ways. Like his parents before him."

Pete tossed his cigarette butt out the open window. "Pick it up, Pierre." This from North.

"Jesus, you're anal. How many trucks have already trampled this site?"

"Make like a good boy scout and pick it up, Pierre."

Pete made an elaborate show of opening the door, getting out, retrieving the end of his smoke from the gathering whiteness and placing it in the ashtray. He dry-washed and spread wide his palms like a cashier in a wicket at a casino. "There, satisfied?"

North ignored this. He extinguished his own in the ashtray and did not ask for another. He turned his attention on Jennifer. "Anything else you can tell us about Mr. Campbell?"

"He was an old man all his life. I mean, that's how he seemed to me. Skinny and bald and a little bent over before he was sixty. He looked much the same into his seventies, the last time I laid eyes on him."

North asked, "Mr. Campbell ever take a farm girl down the aisle?"

"Not his thing or he never found a woman who'd have him." Jennifer shook her head. She had small gold studs in her earlobes. "His parents left him about 200 acres. He farmed the old way, with one ancient Oliver tractor after the horses died. But that doesn't pay the taxes, so he rented out the land and carried on."

North wondered how the man had stood it, living alone. Especially during the long winters. He asked Jennifer if she'd seen him any place except church.

"When I was a teenager, we sneaked back here a few times. It was a great road to go parking at night. He'd freak out if he caught us on his property."

"Parking?" Pete snorted.

Jennifer said, "You should try it. Might loosen you up a bit, although it usually requires a partner."

Before this went further, North said, "Is there anything you're aware of that might have got this Campbell killed? Any family or neighbourly disputes?"

"God, no. Not Hughie."

"And he wasn't queer?"

"Who knows?" Jennifer shrugged.

Pete said, "We should check the files, see if there's an outstanding warrant for animal husbandry."

Jennifer laughed, "That's so not funny."

North said, with some exasperation, "Either of you teenagers notice anything else?"

"Glass fragments out near the silo." Pete took out his cigarette pack, put it away, yawned and stretched from his shoulders to his boots. "On top of the snowmobile tracks. I took some samples."

"Could you tell anything? Type of glass?"

"Heavy glass, maybe headlight shards."

Jennifer said, "Any blood?"

"Nothing." Pete shook his head. "Man, I could use a large double double. Somebody was serious, weren't they? This wasn't a normal domestic."

North nodded in agreement. "One man shot, one apparently not. Maybe we can get a positive ID on Hugh Campbell from dental records."

Jennifer said, "Neither Hughie nor his dad would waste their money on a dentist. Chewed tobacco, both of them. There was a country theory that it killed the pain in their gums and controlled the infection. They wore their teeth down to the stubs."

"Any other identification?"

"No jewellery or watches. There was a wallet near the older man. Leather, burned, nothing in it."

North said, "So it had been cleaned out."

"Probably. Maybe a neighbour can identify somebody, even in that burned condition." Pete shifted in his seat, seemed anxious to leave the vehicle.

Jennifer said, "Could the other man have died from smoke inhalation?"

"What was he doing here? He didn't just fire a .22 and lie down beside the guy to die?"

"As you boys might say, I have no friggin' idea."

"Maybe somebody was killed somewhere else," North said, "and transported here."

"Might explain the snowmobiles," Pete said. "From the tracks, it looked like one of them was pulling a sled." Pale yellow headlights bobbed through thin snow whipping across the road. "And I'll bet that's the coroner."

"Henry Shaw told me it would be an idea to bring in the dogs." North said, "They might be able to help detect the accelerant. He contacted his friends in the Fire Marshall's office. I'm expecting sniffer dogs here any minute."

North left his car and snapped the flap of his parka snugly under his chin. He wanted to go home, crawl into bed and stay there. Or hop a plane to Mexico and not come back until March. Not for the first time since his separation, he experienced a sudden longing—to take Connie with him.

In an attempt to dispel his bleakness, North shrugged his shoulders. He needed to move and to stay in motion. A few hours of sifting, observing, classifying, hoping for a lucky break or a solid lead—that would be good for him.

For starters, it looked as if the coroner had brought trays of Tim Hortons coffee.

CHAPTER 3

As people entered St. Thomas from the west, the first thing they saw was the enormous grey ass of Jumbo up the hill on the right. The elephant had been killed on the railroad tracks of The Railway City and immortalized, life-sized, in concrete. The second landmark was a strip bar called the Amber Lee, owned by bikers. It was the sole peeler bar in town, now that Saint Tease had burned. The St. Thomas force kept an eye on both clubs, but so far the only successful prosecutions had been for parking violations.

Across from the Amber Lee on Talbot Street was the west-end Tim Hortons. It stayed open limited hours on New Year's Day. At 9:30 a.m., North carried a tray of coffees and toasted bagels to a table. In addition to three plain clothes officers regrouping after the fire, the donut shop was hosting post-New Year's revellers and developmentally disabled or mentally ill people who lived in cheap apartments—some of them firetraps—in the area.

North, Jennifer and Pete passed a few minutes in stunned silence, sipping coffee and restoring carbohydrate levels. North's eyes ached. He closed them and they burned. He blinked several times, wiped tears away and glanced through the window. In the east, the sun hovered, white-yellow and cold. Across Talbot Street, a large man in a parka exited the Amber Lee, closed since 1:00 a.m.

North yawned. "Maybe it's just me, but I wish we had more to go on."

Jennifer set down her buttered bagel and licked her thumb and forefinger. "I'll be interested in the full report from the Fire Department. But we're almost positive the farmhouse was torched."

"A safe bet it wasn't teenagers getting their kicks." Pete took a noisy sip of coffee. He knuckled his eyeballs; they looked alcoholic-red and painful. "Let's say somebody was trying to get rid of the bodies. Might have worked if the call hadn't come in so fast."

"Tough to totally destroy a body in a house fire." North said. "Jen-Jen, you found a possible incendiary device at the scene?"

"A melted plastic blob dropped through the floorboards below the kitchen. It was a farm and diesel makes a decent accelerant."

Pete tilted his white ceramic cup and swirled the last remains. He didn't seem to like what he saw, but he finished the drink. "How'd we do with the footprints?"

"The Ident officer and I tried to get a casting, but our mould broke," Jennifer said. "Give us a little more than the photos, but it won't do much in court."

Jennifer stood and stretched. North was careful to look away from breasts lifting high and taut under her shirt. Pete was staring.

"Hughie hated snowmobilers violating his property," Jennifer said. "I'm going to the little girls' room. The next round's on me."

Sitting in the chair, North was so tired, he swayed. It took all his concentration to remain upright.

Jennifer brought new coffees in white cups.

"Those snowmobile tracks near the house and out by the silo, leading back to the ravines," Pete said. "We got some good pictures. There was a sled behind one of them."

North said, "What do you think it all means?"

Pete said, "If I wasn't half asleep, I'd have it figured out, Gumper."

"Tomorrow, why don't you run those photographs to the snowmobile shops here and in London? Find out if anybody can match the tracks."

"Hey, Sarge, can I go home to bed now?" The pouting in Jennifer's tone sounded more like tiredness than banter.

"Take me with you, and you'll have the Happiest New Year ever."

North said, "Pete..."

Hands up, palms forward, small smile. "I'm kidding, she knows I'm kidding."

Jennifer patted Pete's arm. "If Peter really becomes a threat, I'll let you know. *After* Marcel feeds his little peter to the wolves." And she laughed. Not seeming in the least tired now. North understood the fitness nuts and the control freaks and the angry women who wanted to be cops. But why had Jennifer chosen policing? A tall brunette. Wavy hair with red highlights. High cheekbones, prominent nose, tanned complexion, as if she had some Native-Canadian ancestry. And happy. That was the part North didn't get, why a woman who seemed so happy had signed up.

North looked at his watch. Ten-thirty in the morning. Exhaustion was warping time. Five minutes seemed like an hour. Or two hours flashed by, and he wondered where they'd gone. "Why don't the two of you head home and get some sleep? And that wasn't an opening for more innuendo, Pierre. Staff Sergeant is away for the stat holiday today, so Constable Skelding and I are meeting with the inspector at 11:00. I hope like hell he didn't usher in the New Year in his usual immaculate style."

"Good luck with that one," Jennifer murmured.

"If the inspector doesn't have any brilliant new ideas for us, I'm calling it a day after that."

"I need a shower, and I'll catch my second wind," Jennifer said. "We should talk to Sarah McKinley, the neighbour who called in the fire. Get that out of the way."

North was the sergeant, but Jen-Jen was setting the agenda. It was probably his worn-out state that made anger flare inside him. It couldn't be related to his sensitivity to the chain of command. It had nothing to do with Connie leaving before Christmas or the hours he'd spent at the casino over the holidays, with predictable results. Nothing to do with blowing the sole holiday visit he'd had with Maddy and Dylan. No connection with the unexpected fury he'd experienced upon seeing his first wife again when he'd picked up his kids in Burlington to take them out for a tawdry Christmas lunch. North waited several seconds before he said, in a quiet voice without looking at her, "That's a good idea, Constable Duchamps."

They were about to leave when North had another thought. "You have access to a snowmobile, Pierre?"

"A friend of mine has an old John Deere that still runs."

"Think you could borrow it for today?"

"Can't you get somebody else?"

"Pretty tough on New Year's Day. I had enough trouble convincing two uniforms to stay at the Campbell place. We need to see where the tracks lead from the farm."

Pete looked sullen.

"A couple of hours won't kill you," North said. "The sun's out. If it goes above freezing, the evidence will melt. Besides..."

Pete finished the sentence for him, "Yeah, yeah... The first 24 hours are crucial."

"You can put in for overtime."

"Fat chance of collecting. I'll do it. So fuck off and leave me alone."

North eyeballed him but let the outburst go. Constable Pete Heemstra stood and surveyed the brown and black café-style tables, now mostly empty. "Even the retards and crazies have enough sense to go home for a nap."

Jennifer laughed, but North didn't think that was very funny, and Pete didn't smile. The bubble of laughter from Jennifer seemed to burst, leaving an uncomfortable silence. Without saying goodbye, Pete stumbled out of the restaurant.

## CHAPTER 4

A tap emitted a steady plop, plop, plop onto stacks of dishes. A large black cat prowled the counter. On the floor near the mat by the door, a marmalade-coloured feline sprawled, licking itself. At the far end of the room, under an octagonal clock with ornate numbers, an enormous green parrot shuttled silently back and forth on a perch.

The air was a rich blend of sour milk, bird feces, dust and damp fur. Leather boots lay twisted and cracked from moisture and use beside manure-crusted rubber boots on a dark blue mat. The officers stamped their feet and bent to remove boots, but Sarah McKinley said, "Don't bother with that."

The kitchen chairs were chrome with cracked plastic seats and dull green backs. Sarah moved two chairs out from a round maple table littered with invoices, books, newspapers and flyers. Jennifer and North removed their parkas and hung them over the backs of neighbouring chairs before sitting. Jennifer extracted a notebook and pen from her breast pocket. After a shower and a change of clothes, Jen-Jen looked like she could go all day.

Sarah wore a denim skirt that settled halfway between knee and ankle. Below the skirt, her thick calves were warmed by long underwear: grey, as were the socks inside her leather sandals. A brocade vest covered much of a T-shirt that had once been white. A leather strap necklace with a wooden cross dangled from her raw, heavily creased neck. Long white hair, with traces of its original red, was braided and rolled into a tight bun at the back. A blue Toronto Maple Leafs ball cap shaded narrow eyes behind thick glasses. She had a straight nose and a heavy jaw. If she'd been a man, she would have been handsome even at her advanced age.

She said, "Happy New Year" to Jennifer and ignored North. "Must be a special occasion. First I get visited by these handsome firefighters. And now the police. You don't honour us with your presence much any more, Jenny. Off to the big city, and you forgets where you come from."

Jennifer smiled. "St. Thomas is the big city?"

Sarah smirked, closed off that expression and squinted briefly at North with blue eyes so pale they seemed distant, milky. "Coldest New Year's I remember. Who's this fella?"

"My boss. Sergeant Carl North of the St. Thomas Police."

Sarah surveyed North up and down and said, "Would youse like a coffee?"

North hesitated and said, "A pick-me-up would be good. We've been up most of the night."

Sarah stared at him as if he were idiotic as she plugged in an electric kettle. She leaned her weight against the counter and cleared her throat loudly three times, found a tissue in her skirt pocket and spat into it. "I suppose this is about Hughie Campbell. God rest his soul, the man was a complete fool to live there by his self the way his mind was going. I told him as much."

North said, "You called 911 when you saw the fire."

"The christly snowmobilers, forgive my French, woke me up. I never sleep the way I used to. Sometimes I'm up two, three times in the night, reads a bit, makes a coffee and goes back to bed."

The kettle screamed. Using the cord, Sarah whipped the plug out of its socket. She spooned instant coffee into mugs, creaming and sugaring to their instructions. She took hers black. When everyone had their caffeine, she plunked herself into a chair.

"So you heard snowmobiles," North said.

"I knew Hughie would be fuming. Once the leaves go, you can see his place real good from here. For whatever godforsaken reason, they stopped by his silo. Both of them."

Jennifer was writing quickly. She said, "Two machines or two people?"

"Both, I guess you'd say. They come from the trails by the ravines and run over where Hughie's barn used to be. With the snow, I didn't have real clean sightlines, but I watched them get off and move around in the headlights. Like they was trying to put something in that old silo. Empty for years. With the ups and downs in the cattle price after mad cow disease, it'll never be used again."

North looked her in the eyes. He found the woman's pale gaze unsettling and shifted his attention to her big-knuckled hands as he asked, "Could you see what they were putting in the silo?"

"I said *trying* to put in the silo. No."

"Any guesses?"

"Seemed to be dragging more than lifting. The headlight on one of the snowmobiles went out."

Jennifer noted this. North asked, "What happened?"

"I heard this crack, like a tree snapping when it's freezing cold. I wonder if Hughie didn't take a pot-shot at them. Wouldn't put it past the old fool. Next thing you know, the snowmobiles are up by his house."

North pulled on Jennifer's sleeve and said quietly, "The glass."

Jennifer nodded.

North said. "The two men left whatever they were dragging out by the silo?"

"Guess so. They moved to the kitchen side, away from me." The woman sipped from her mug, rolling the liquid around in her mouth before swallowing. "I heard some loud noises, maybe inside Hughie's house. I fetch my thirty-ought-six out of the cellar just in case, but they headed back to the ravine. Maybe ten or fifteen minutes later, after I put the gun away and finish my coffee, I see this glow, like fire and smoke with it. Going pretty good when I call 911."

The parrot squawked. The woman told it to shut up. It replied, "Shut up, shut up," and shunted on its perch before heeding its own instruction.

North couldn't imagine any man living with Sarah. Being around her made him wonder, again, why he couldn't bring himself to reconcile with Connie, a woman devoted to making a good home; neat, endlessly supportive. Why had he driven her away? He snapped out of his reverie by asking, "So this thirty-ought-six rifle, you have it registered?"

Sarah's expression said she'd shoot him if he posed that question again. Heat rose inside him. He said, "You realize it's a criminal offence to fail to cooperate with a police officer."

Sarah turned to Jennifer. "I thought police officers had to be at least six foot."

North was half way out of his chair when he felt Jennifer's hand on his arm. She said, "How long was it, from the time the snowmobiles went up to the house until you saw the fire?"

"Half, three quarters of an hour."

"That bundle, did they take that away with them?"

The woman shrugged her shoulders under her T-shirt and vest. North felt his voice rising and didn't try to control it, "Did they or didn't they?"

"Can't be positive."

"Was there anything about the drivers you would recognize if you saw them again?"

"I wouldn't know them if they tried to rape me standing up in my own kitchen with the lights on." The old woman hooted out a laugh that startled the cats and the police officers and carried no mirth. Her face immediately resumed its masculine placidity.

North didn't know what to say and apparently, neither did Jennifer. After an embarrassing pause, Sarah eyed North. "Surprised me, you didn't ask if you could have a cigarette with your coffee."

"I quit, more or less."

"Didn't stay quit, from the smell off ya. You should give it up. It killed my Iain, back in '69. He was barely 48. Me and the boys carried on for a while. Now there's just me." Laughter rumbled out of her and quit.

Jennifer closed her notebook. "How are the boys?"

"Never see Jock. Moved to Vancouver years ago. A partner, no wife, who knows what that means? Poor Reggie went off the railway bridge in '66, before you was born. Weaker than his father and until I got the news, suicide never crossed my mind. If it had, I might have tried to do something."

Jennifer's voice was soft and warm. "I was thinking more of Duncan. He's known to the police."

"Known to the police." Sarah stopped as if contemplating the weakness of men in her family before continuing. "We had Duncan after Reggie died, a surprise to some people. I was 40, and the neighbours thought Iain had hung his tools in the shed long before."

"When I was a kid, I had a crush on Duncan." Jennifer smiled. "I must have been nine or 10."

"A good looking boy. But no Iain." Sarah's chapped lips spread in a forced leer. "One thing about my husband, he had the looks. Duncan has some of that, though too much of his mother in the looks department."

"One time Duncan came to pick up weaner pigs." Jennifer was drawing out her words, pausing after some of her sentences, as if the act of sitting in this kitchen, conversing with Sarah, were pulling her back to her roots. "Mom and Dad had him in for coffee. He rode me on his shoulders from the barn. I was the queen of the rodeo. Him and his red hair."

"Never seen a family with such difference as my boys. One dark-haired, one blond and Duncan with the real old-time Scotch red. Like they was all sired off a different bull, which they wasn't. And none of 'em with any inclination to farm."

"Duncan still come around?"

"Once in a blue moon. Must have been one this past Christmas Eve. He shows up with a couple of buddies and some women, about as rough a crowd as you'd ever come across. Tattoos and the whole nine yards. Doesn't stay long. They drinks me out of house and home. You making these inquiries for personal reasons?"

North said, "Duncan McKinley's known to us."

"Got a few things to tend to in the barn." The woman used thick old arms to hoist herself from the table. She narrowed her eyes. "Known to you, eh? He got in with a bad crowd. Like his father, but wilder. Never found a woman to settle him down. One thing I'll say for both him and his dad. They could make me laugh."

As North and Jennifer prepared to leave, North said, "We have a favour to ask. We need a positive identification on the body of Hughie Campbell. He's at the Elgin General today, waiting for an autopsy."

"Suppose somebody has to do it. Wouldn't want him going down to an unmarked grave."

"It's not always easy to identify a burn victim."

"Guess I'll either know him or I won't. You have some Indian blood in you?"

The question, winging in out of nowhere, startled North. "What makes you say that?"

"Your colouring. You're kinda puny and fine-boned to be Native, but looks like there might be some in your ancestry."

"My grandmother was an Alberta Cree."

Sarah clucked her tongue, twice. "There's good in 'em. If you can keep 'em off the hooch. Had some here from Muncey. Worked for me if you want to call that work. You've got your Daylight Savings and your Standard Time. Then there's Native Time."

"I ought to…"

Again, North felt Jennifer's hand on his forearm. "Sergeant North and I are here to investigate two deaths. And I think we've about wrapped that up."

As they made their way to the door, past the marmalade cat, Sarah chuckled, laced her thick fingers together over her middle and said to the parrot. "Not too tough to get a rise out of some people." The green bird was raucous in agreement.

**CHAPTER 5**

"How are you feeling?"

"The chemo was no fun. But I'm okay."

"What does okay mean?"

"Still get tired."

"After last night, your ass must be dragging. Maybe we shouldn't be doing this."

"I had a nap. I feel like a new man."

"That explains it. I didn't have time for a nap, and I feel like an old man." North reached for a silver cigarette package and thought better of it when the fire investigator gave him a disapproving look. He put the smokes away and said, "Sorry, Henry."

"I heard you quit."

"I did. I just didn't stay quit."

"Look where that road goes: chemo and an uncertain future. One good thing, I don't worry as much as I used to. Every day's a new one."

"Thanks for coming on a stat holiday. Anything you can give me will be a big help." North was in his favourite chair, a battered recliner in his apartment at Grand Central. The chair had been with him longer than his two wives.

Henry Shaw was sitting on the couch, under a large print of Canadian mountains and evergreens in winter. The fire investigator was wearing his usual blue uniform. He smiled and said, "You know I can't say anything official about the fires."

"Official is for officials." North sipped from a Ford mug that contained cooling coffee, murky with milk. He made a face and set the cup down. "People like you and me, we know the main thing is to get the overall gist of things. There'll be more than enough official when we get to the paper-work."

"And there's never enough of that. Okay, the sniffer dogs were a big help at the Campbell fire. We also tried them at Saint Tease. Less help there."

"What did they find at Campbell's?"

"Diesel. A very common accelerant."

"You sure?"

Henry smiled and pulled at his thin bottom lip. "The dogs were."

North waved his cigarette package. "Do you mind?"

Henry hesitated. One hand jerked toward the package, before he slapped his wrist and laughed. "Truth is, I'd love to join you. Doctors won't let me, and they might have a point."

North left his chair and crossed the room to open a heavy curtain that ran ceiling to floor before undoing the latch on a patio door to a snowy balcony. He grunted as he yanked on the door, sliding it to the side a couple of inches. "Must have frozen."

He was facing east. Afternoon sunlight sparkled off the roof of the building next door. North closed his eyes. Colours danced among the black. He opened them again and removed a duMaurier from the package. He turned back to the darker room as he lit it. "And the fire started—or was started—in the kitchen, where we found the two bodies."

"Not much doubt about that, from the v-pattern on the walls."

North inhaled, held it and blew smoke toward the open crack in the door. Henry was right. He shouldn't be doing this. He should never have started again. He should butt out right now. He took another drag. "Were you able to reconstruct what transpired there?"

"The report won't be finished for a bit. But we're 99 percent sure both men were dead before the fire was set."

"Old farmhouse would go up, just like that." North snapped his fingers. "But apparently they left plenty of evidence."

"Gas makes a great flash fire and a terrific explosion if properly vaporized. Favoured by arsonists everywhere... but it doesn't have the properties of diesel fuel for something like a house fire."

North moved back to his chair, drew on his cigarette and butted it in a dirty ashtray on a stool by his coffee cup. Henry was still talking. "It soaks into clothing, floorboards, even skin. It burns, rather than exploding. A fire can really spread in wood coated with diesel. More smoke at the beginning, granted, and it takes longer to get going, but once it does..." The man seemed momentarily somewhere else, as if imagining an arsonist spreading accelerant around an old farm kitchen.

Henry shifted his hips on the couch, coughed, took a shallow breath and asked for water.

North ran the tap in the kitchen until cold and brought him a glass. "Thanks," Henry gasped. He took a sip, then a longer drink, settled back on the couch and continued in a voice that sounded strained. "The thing about getting sick is, don't do it."

North smiled and nodded.

"I hate that term, cancer survivor. For one thing, who knows if you are? I've got one less lung than I used to."

"One day at a time, Henry. Isn't that how we're all supposed to live?"

"Thanks. Nice to know somebody who's half Jesus, half Gandhi."

"Just trying to help." North grinned and made the sign of the cross. "Anything else about the fire?"

"Not a professional job. Whoever set it underestimated the degree of heat and the amount of time it takes to cremate a body, that's if you want to destroy an adult. Or in this case, two bodies. But they were smart enough to leave a door open."

North shifted in his chair and looked out the window at his concrete balcony and the tops of wintry-looking buildings beyond. "Thereby letting in snow and moisture. How intelligent was that?"

"Oxygen."

"How do you know a door was left open?"

"The burn pattern on the floor. And somebody smashed a kitchen window. Clean glass outside, no soot, so it was broken by somebody, not blown out by the fire."

North wanted another cigarette. He stood, paced, ran his fingers through his hair. He sucked on his false front tooth and inhaled cool air streaming through the crack in the patio door, before sliding it shut. "Anything else about the bodies?"

"You know the bigger guy, not the one who was shot, the other one? We think he was burned twice."

"How the hell can you tell that?"

"We're pretty sure both bodies were there before the fire started. The burn pattern on the floor around the bodies supports that idea. But the big guy, he had burn patterns on his back, where it was touching the floor."

"Which means?"

"Either he was burned on the back and then rolled over, which seems crazy to me. Or he had burn damage to his back when somebody put him in the house. Like, maybe those guys on snowmobiles."

North ran a finger down his nose and fondled the indentation where it had been broken. "Might the big guy show more burn damage because his body fat acted as a fuel?"

Henry coughed wetly, took a sip of water and wiped his eyes. "Not sure this fire burned long enough for that. And not on his back."

"That fire at Saint Tease, you still think it was natural gas?"

Henry asked if he could use the bathroom before they got into that. North told him where it was. "I hope there's clean towels," North called to Henry's slim back before he disappeared.

North opened the patio door a bit and lit another smoke while he waited.

Henry yawned twice when he returned. As he took his place on the couch, he rubbed his eyes. "I'll sleep like a baby tonight. That other fire at the strip club was natural gas. Accidental, as far as we can tell."

"No evidence of arson."

Henry shook his head. "But here's the thing. Natural gas is a great way to hide arson. It was an old building. Natural gas is lighter than air. It can build up, go to the ceiling and then travel or gradually come down and fill a room until it's ignited by something as innocent as a pilot light. Nobody has to be there."

"Saint Tease reopened not that long ago. It would have been inspected."

"When you inspect, you don't take down all the drywall and check every inch," Henry smiled. "And sometimes people are supposed to do things in an inspection they simply don't do."

"Was it a furnace problem?"

"They used gas stoves in the kitchen. Natural gas dryers in a room down the hall. Apparently all this was left over from the days when it was a hotel with regular guests, and they had both kitchen and laundry facilities. That's going back a few years."

"As far as we know, nobody was staying overnight. They had a licence to sell booze, and they brought in the peelers and that was it." North reached for another cigarette and stopped himself. The apartment had a sparse, neglected feeling. It lacked Connie's gentle touches, an airing and a good cleaning. "The thing about Saint Tease, there's a possible motive for arson."

"You really got it in your head there could have been a firebug?"

North lifted his shoulders and spread his palms. "The Pythons own the Amber Lee. Our information suggests they were not thrilled with a freelancer going after a share of the peeler market. And the big guy at the farmhouse was burned twice. Maybe the first time was at Saint Tease."

"True. But without evidence to connect the dots, that's sheer specu-lation."

North said, "You should get a job teaching at the Ontario Police College."

<h2 style="text-align:center">CHAPTER 6</h2>

The air was stuffy. The police station was over-crowded, a story that kept making headlines in the *St. Thomas Times-Journal*. But city council never seemed to find the budget to build a new one. The Criminal Investigations meeting had been called by Staff Sergeant Norval Vandenberg. It was the day after New Year's. Vandenberg's email said the 9:00 a.m. start, an hour later than the usual officers' meeting, would give people time to catch up on calls and paperwork after the holiday. "A holiday for some," North had muttered.

Staff Sergeant Vandenberg had served with Canadian Forces in Cyprus and entered police work with his military bearing and his dark, thick moustache intact. He started the meeting at 0858 hours in a pale room with pale lime green stacking chairs, unstacked around tables butted together, boardroom-style.

"Paperwork is critical to every investigation. When we do a good job on the paperwork, the rest falls into place."

Without looking, North knew that Constable Pete Heemstra would be lip-synching in exaggerated Dutch/German to the nearest constable. "Ven ve do ein gutter yob mit der paperverk..."

The staff sergeant reviewed everything officers knew about the two New Year's Eve fires. The fact that there were two in one night, he called "unusual for this area." There could be a connection between the two blazes. "We have no identity, as yet, on the other deceased we are assum-ing is male. Unless you have more information, Sergeant North?"

"Not yet." North sipped coffee and tried not to think about nicotine. His wrist was better today, after the fall on the ice at the Campbell farm. "But I'd like to hear Constable Heemstra's report from yesterday on the snowmobile tracks at the scene."

Dark brown circles shaded to green under Pete's vacant eyes. He checked his notepad and cleared his throat. "Emergency vehicles played hell with the evidence in the yard, but I borrowed an old John Deere snowmobile and followed the tracks."

"Nothing runs like a Heemstra," murmured Dexter Phillips to muted laugher. Constable Phillips referred to himself as the force's contribution to multiculturalism. He was born on the Oneida of the Thames Reserve northwest of St. Thomas and traced his ancestry to the Iroquois Confederacy.

"This is not the Comedy Network," Staff Sergeant Vandenberg said.

Looking too hung-over for a snappy comeback, Pete concentrated on his notes. "I followed tracks from the Campbell farm back to the ravine. They'd show up here and there, and then you'd lose them in the drifts. From where they entered and left the field, I'd say they came from town and exited the other way, heading west."

"You have evidence to corroborate that?"

"I took pictures. I wonder if they were dropping off the body of Mystery Man, the dead guy who wasn't shot. The tracks looked deeper when the machines were arriving than when they were leaving. I called around this morning to see whether we could ID the make or model of the machine from the tracks themselves. Apparently that's not possible."

"The deceased were both males?"

"From the bone structure and the traces of clothing, it looks like a slam dunk on the gender."

"Thank you for that and for completing the work on New Year's Day."

Pete said, "Happy New Year, one and all." North could almost feel the pain rotating inside the man's skull as Pete added, "My invoice for over-time is in the mail."

Staff Sergeant Vandenberg reminded Pete that he was to attend the autopsy at the St. Thomas Elgin General Hospital later that day. The staff sergeant flipped a sheet on his clipboard and turned to Carl North. "Anything further from your visit to this neighbour, one Sarah McKinley?"

North said, "We did get an identification on Hugh Campbell last night. Sarah recognized his belt buckle. Apparently he always wore the same belt."

"Not conclusive, then."

"No, but he wasn't burned as badly as the other guy. He was the right size, and Sarah recognized his face, or what was left of it. We'll compare blood, old bone breaks and any organ abnormalities from the autopsy with his medical records."

"Anything else from this neighbour?"

Jennifer Duchamps smiled with regular, white teeth, as North nodded in her direction. "Constable Duchamps was raised in the area west of the Campbell fire, and was acquainted with both the farmer and the neighbour who called it in. Anything to add to my report, Constable Duchamps?"

"Not at this time, Sir."

Ductwork growled as a fresh blast of heat entered a room North found already short of oxygen. He said, "The neighbour's son, Duncan McKinley rides with the Pythons, a motorcycle gang with a meeting place in this area."

Staff Sergeant Vandenberg said, "The OPP says the gang uses a farm north and west of Shedden."

The previous summer, with the cooperation of the Ontario Provincial Police, North and Constable Skelding had stopped in at that farm, following up on allegations of running a common bawdy house at the Amber Lee. The allegations had gone nowhere; the complaints swiftly withdrawn. He remembered a white frame farmhouse, not in the best of shape, a barn and a shed with motorcycles. A huge fire pit. An elaborate gate guarding the entrance to the laneway off the road. "This Duncan appeared at Sarah McKinley's place on or around Christmas with a group of friends who sounded like bikers. This is probably straight coincidence, but Constable Heemstra says the snowmobiles may have headed west on the trails from the farm. That's toward the Iona/Shedden area."

"It's 10 miles to Shedden as the snowmobile flies," Staff Sergeant Vandenberg said. "And the machines could have been heading for Shedden or Detroit or Calgary. Hardly enough for us to justify a warrant or even picking up McKinley for questioning."

"I'm aware of that, Sir."

"If you're telling me he's worth keeping an eye on, I would agree."

"Thank you, Sir. Constable Duchamps has a photo of a boot imprint from the scene."

A piece of cardboard covered the lens of an LED projector. Jennifer removed this cardboard to project slides on a wall. She showed photos of a boot imprint and a split casting. The tread pattern of one boot was distinctive. Her department would be circulating a photograph to footwear stores, looking for the manufacturer.

"You can see the wear on the heel of the boot." She switched to a photograph of the casting. "We're seeing a hole right here." With a red laser pointer, she circled an area in the middle of a photograph of the casting of the boot sole. "Looks like a puncture. And there's a crack here." Jennifer indicated the general area with the pointer.

The staff sergeant said the retailer could sometimes be narrowed down geographically, perhaps to a London area store. Sometimes not.

North added, "And don't forget the glass shards. A neighbour confirms a .22 was fired before the blaze was set. We're looking for a snowmobile that's missing a headlight."

Vandenberg consulted his papers and turned to Constable Dexter Phillips, "Any indication of what started the Saint Tease fire?"

"I was called to a service station robbery, so I left Constable Skelding in charge." Dexter nodded to a tall officer in his twenties with a sandy blond moustache as full as the staff sergeant's. North had had a good experience with Tom Skelding when they investigated the bikers and later, on some preliminary work around drug trafficking in St. Thomas. He had talked to Tom at different times about possibly transferring to Criminal Investigations. The Skeldings had invited North over twice for drinks and a back yard barbecue.

"Place ignited like a matchbox." Constable Phillips leaned back in his chair, yawned and his dark brown eyes watered. "Twenty minutes, and she was toast. Old frame hotel south of the ravine lands, converted to a strip bar 14 months ago."

"Any injuries?"

"All those sweet girls escaped with no clothes on their backs. And not much on their fronts. Our brothers from the fire department were happy to offer blankets."

The staff sergeant said, absolutely deadpan, "And hot soup. And a warm bed. And I did not say that. Did you speak with any of these young women? Or any bar patrons?"

"I was kidding. The place was closed when the fire started. But Constable Skelding, you talked to two women."

Constable Tom Skelding coughed into his hand. He looked pale and tired, as if the holidays had taken a toll. His fingers were trembling, and he shifted in his chair. He couldn't seem to get comfortable. But he grinned as he said, "A tough assignment, but somebody has to do it. My main interview was with a woman whose stage name is Candy. Her driver's license identified her as Ivana Genska from Mississauga. The name is Slovakian, and we are checking with Immigration."

"Are her documents genuine?"

"Her driver's license appears to be. She has an Ontario health card. She's on the circuit, dancing at the Amber Lee this week, Saint Tease in the past. And I would like to say, I did not have sex with that woman."

Tom smiled in appreciation of the chorus that erupted.

"Thank you, Mr. President."

"A likely story, Gelding."

"Give a real man the assignment."

With a straight face, Tom added, "Sir, a shivering stripper at 20 below? I was able to restrain myself."

"Most grateful you took the moral high ground, Constable."

Tom rubbed his left eye. His skin was mottled. He was slumping in his chair. "Candy was unable to get upstairs to retrieve her things, due to the intensity of the heat and smoke."

"So rooms upstairs were in use?"

"Sometimes, girls stayed over. The building is owned by Abe Friesen, who lives on Aldborough. I checked with land registry at 8:30 this morning. This Friesen purchased the building almost two years ago for some seventy thousand dollars."

Staff Sergeant Vandenberg raised dark eyebrows. "How'd he get the business for seventy thousand?"

"Our information is that it was in poor condition. It had been vacant for some time."

"Have we had any dealings with this Abe Friesen or his bar?"

"One LCBO infraction early on. Apparently that was quickly rectified."

"So Mr. Friesen is clean?"

"Strictly speaking, squeaky clean," Tom answered with some hesitation. "Hard to say what to think when you meet the gentleman. Over the past year, we did respond to one citizen complaint involving lap dancing and operating a common bawdy house. A little undercover investigation turned up some questions but no charges. I talked to Mr. Friesen, the night of the fire."

"How did he seem?"

"More shaken than stirred. The man was close to tears at one point," Tom said. "We don't know yet if Mr. Friesen was experiencing financial problems. He has a steady day job at the Ford plant. Made a point of letting us know he was a family man. Until his wife left him and took the kids. Not sure whether or not that separation is connected to his recent line of business."

North liked the background information Tom had found out so quickly. In support of what the constable was saying, North added, "Family men don't usually open strip clubs."

"Claimed to be fulfilling a lifelong ambition." Tom was looking ill. "He's young, late twenties, early thirties."

Dexter checked his notebook. "St. Thomas already had too much coffee, that's what he said."

To make sure everybody was clear on this, North said, "The other strip club is owned by a numbered company, but the Pythons hold the paper."

Dexter shrugged massive shoulders and pressed his lips together as he checked his notes. "We understand they have controlling interest in the Amber Lee as well as a tattoo parlour and a massage place or whatever you call it on the edge of town. And title to two buildings on Talbot Street."

Staff Sergeant Vandenberg asked, "Houses of ill repute?"

"Appears to be legit." Tom spread his hands wide. "They rent to businesses on the main floor. Apartments on the upper floors. Mr. Friesen claimed to be shocked by the fire. But," Tom flipped pages and stopped when he found something, "I heard him say to one of the girls, 'They told me they would get me.'"

Tom placed large hands on the table in front of him and leaned forward. "Later, he denied saying it. We questioned the stripper. She thought us police officers might enjoy sexual intercourse with ourselves."

North erupted in laughter and was joined by others. The staff sergeant said, "I assume you did not succumb to that temptation."

Constable Skelding scraped back his chair and thrust his legs in front of him. He linked his fingers behind his head. That stopped their trembling. "I asked Friesen what he was afraid of. He said he wasn't afraid. Went back to the line about just getting his business going. All the trouble he's having."

"One more thing," Dexter added. "A neighbour claims a vehicle was spotted entering the parking lot of Saint Tease a few minutes before the fire erupted. An SUV."

"Anything on make, model, licence plate, ID of the driver?"

"Nothing like that, sorry."

Vandenberg asked North whether he had any final words. North straightened in his chair. At five feet eight inches, he often felt dwarfed by the others, a feeling enhanced by the cramped quarters for the meeting. "The Fire Marshall's report could take three weeks, longer if things get complicated. We need to identify the second deceased at the farmhouse and we need the autopsy results on both bodies. We'll talk to Abe Friesen and have a go at the Pythons. Plus, keep our eyes open for this mysterious SUV."

The staff sergeant stroked his moustache. "What's your focus?"

North thought, cigarettes, and I need one, badly. He looked directly at the staff sergeant and said, "I'll have a crack at this Candy. See if she can help us make some sense out of this mess."

CHAPTER 7

A woman with long slim legs sauntered toward North and Dexter on a carpet that had once been purple. She was wearing red bikini bottoms, red heels and one red and white garter. The auburn nipples of her small breasts were the size of silver dollars. One was pierced with a small barbell.

"Is police, no?" she asked. "But why no uniform?"

"Maybe we should get you a uniform," North chuckled and folded his arms across his chest. "You look cold."

The woman pouted. Pink lipstick curved above and below her lips. She had sculptured cheekbones, an East European accent. "Do not to spoil this moment. I like man in uniform. Little bit horny for this man." And she smiled. The smile did not reach blue eyes defined by pink false eyelashes.

North smiled back at her. "Much as I wish I had time, we're on police business."

"With this one, I play the cowboy and the Indian." She pulled at the sleeve of Dexter's dark jacket. "Handsome mens, they turn me on. Two handsome mens together, they makes me horny as dogs, no?"

As she was saying this, her eyes shifted to the entrance behind the officers. In dark parkas, two grinning men who looked like truck drivers closed the door on a gust of cold air and steam.

"Another time, sweetheart," Dexter said. "The sign says Candy is dancing today?"

The woman's eyes glazed over, and she nodded curtly. "Down the hall, gentlemens. New guest for to greet."

Her left hand found North's forearm. "You have beautiful, beautiful eye. I am mad woman for beautiful eye. Yes."

It was a minor shock, but North realized he was moved by the woman's gesture. His arm tingled, briefly, at her touch.

The woman gyrated her red-bikinied bottom toward the newcomers. A snake pattern had been tattooed in the centre of an intricate pattern above her narrow buttocks.

North's eyes moved back to Dexter, who cocked a wrist and waved his fingers. "You have the beautiful eye. I am mad blond woman in love, yes?"

North told Dexter to fuck off, and followed him to the bar, where men had come in for lunch at round tables, alone or in groups. A few had drinks and burgers with crispy fries. Most just had drinks. Three bare-breasted women, one slim and athletic, the second more Rubenesque, the third a petite woman with a French maid's apron and netted stockings, worked the room.

On the stage to North's immediate right, a stripper with enlarged breasts that betrayed no bounce swayed her round ass back and forth to a pounding disco remix. The woman's hair brushed a chrome pole she was clenching. Her fingernails were long and red. She was half bent over. Her back was arched for maximum rear extension.

With mincing steps, the French maid escorted a man in a business jacket to one of three private cubicles with pink curtains. A younger man, his baseball cap on backwards, followed this with hungry eyes. More experienced patrons pretended not to notice.

North's vision was adjusting to the contrasting dark and light of the place and barely avoided a leg extended by a bearded, big-bellied man drinking at a table with another man. North took one quick step to right his balance.

The big-bellied man chuckled and winked at his drinking buddy who had a reddish beard and a pirate's kerchief covering much of his red hair. On the back of the larger man's dark green leather vest, an embroidered snake twisted in a half circle beneath the word Pythons. A second patch curved beneath the larger one. It said, "Ride Free Or Die."

North shifted his right hand toward his holster. "What's so funny, Turk?"

"The smaller the cop, the harder they fall." Turk's voice was deep, with a slight lisp. He sounded less threatening than he looked. "No little cop girls available to case the bars?"

Dexter's face seemed to darken. "You gentlemen got some lip on you, for citizens who just assaulted a police officer."

The red-haired man smiled at the table. "Health and safety violation number 3601—customer trips on table leg."

North moved in close to the larger man. Dexter stepped back, giving him room. "You own this dive, Turk?"

With the back of one broad hand, the man rubbed his cheek. "Numbered company, far as I know." The man's grin creased the flesh of his face into rounded folds. His sleeves were rolled up on muscular fore-arms. A snake tattoo curled down his hairy right arm, its tongue seeming to flick near his wide right thumb.

"I thought you 'Ride Free Or Die' dudes believed in free enterprise."

"You are making no sense, my friend."

"The fire at Saint Tease, I hear you were trying to limit competition."

Turk's eyes held steadily on North's. His lisp was slightly more pro-nounced as he said, "We know anything about Saint Tease, Dunc?"

"Not a goddamn thing." Dunc was grinning. "And the less we know about that shit-hole, the better."

The music had shifted to a pulsing techno beat. Dexter asked, "What should we do with these guys?"

"If we put a bullet in the red-headed stranger, do you think the department would approve the expense?"

"Hey," Duncan said. His smile faded, his face paled.

"Can't do that, Sergeant North." Dexter's tone sounded bureaucratic. "Not without a warrant."

"Okay, get one. While we're waiting, ask him which dancer is Candy?"

Turk opened his arms like a circus barker and shouted, "They all are, let me tell you." He glanced around and said, "Try the door-greeter. She's working the floor at the moment."

"We understand she's an expert on what happened at Saint Tease. She was there."

Turk looked like he couldn't care less what North understood. "Private dances start at 25 bucks, if that puts lead in your pencil. Though I suppose pigs like you are looking for freebies."

"Why would you be promoting private dances?" North asked. "I thought you didn't have any interest in the place."

"Wouldn't be sitting here, if I wasn't interested."

North shifted his gaze to the red-haired man. "You're Duncan McKinley, aren't you?"

"His handle's Studs," Turk said. "Because he really knows how to hammer 'em. Right, Studsly?" The men high-fived and thumb-gripped each other and turned to their beer.

North snapped a toonie on a neighbouring table and said to Dexter, "Why don't you order yourself a coffee? Keep an eye on those two prospective felons while I interview Candy."

"If you're not back in 10, I'm sending in the cavalry. And the Health Unit."

North saluted. "Thanks, Dex," and signalled to Candy, who was serving a single glass of draft to a senior. Patches of white beard grew like hoar frost across the old man's skinny face and neck.

Like a European model exaggerating her figure, Candy strolled over to North.

"Yes, beautiful brown eye?"

"Snake Man says it's 25 for a private session."

Her blues eyes widened. She leaned toward his ear, her voice soft. "Private dancer for you? I am more horny all the time."

The curtained cubicle with the pink curtain had a triangular black-padded bench in one corner. A solid, black, metal table stood about two feet in front of it. "Only private dance for you?"

"Do I have a choice?"

The woman's mascara-rimmed eyes narrowed as she smiled and said, "Lap dance is 50. For handsome police, maybe some deal."

He extracted a 20 and 10 from his wallet. "Instead, let's talk for 30."

The woman tucked the bills into the elastic of her bikini bottom and shimmied her upper body. "Talk with mens, this can be very sexy."

"I need you to talk about something besides sex. Or maybe there's a connection. I understand you were at Saint Tease the night it burned." North patted the black vinyl top of the bench.

She eased onto the bench beside him, crossed her strong, bare legs and yawned. "Excuse. Candy work very hard for money. What is it you want, from Saint Tease club?"

North decided to begin again. "What's a beautiful woman like you doing in a business like this?"

The woman smiled and said. "Is what I do. Is not life."

The music switched to Abba with a strong Latin beat. The woman snapped her fingers. "This is the music I like. I dance for you, yes?"

"Maybe some other time, Ivana."

"You know my name?"

"You'd be surprised what I know. The night Saint Tease burned, you were there."

The woman's head bobbed in agreement, her eyes widening again, alive with fear. She glanced at the curtain and then at the concrete floor near North's feet.

"Abe Friesen apparently said something about somebody out to get him."

The dancer's head rose and fell in agreement. No eye contact with North as he said, "Do you know what he meant?"

Candy's hair shifted to reveal silver, hoop earrings as she shook her head, no.

"We have contacts in Immigration. My fellow officers tell me your driver's license appears to be in order, but what about your immigration papers?"

She looked right at North and said, "You are not this man who should ask. Citizen of this country, like you."

"You have the papers to prove it?"

"They keep papers, these mens. I have, but they keep."

North said gently, "So you have to stay in the business. As long as they say. And who is 'they?'"

"Mens. Not so different here, not like I think, when we come."

"Are these the men who said they would get Abe Friesen?"

The woman's gaze darted about, like that of an animal, trapped in a cage. If desperate mammals would chew off their own body parts to escape, what was wrong with displaying your body, using it to stay alive? The woman's fear and vulnerability stirred other longings and instincts inside North. She hadn't answered his question so he said, "You know who threatened the owner, but you're afraid to say."

"I know nothing."

"Our dance time must be up. Here's my card." He dug one out of his shirt pocket, found a pen and added a number. "If you remember something or find yourself in need of police protection, call me on my cell. Leave a message if I'm not answering."

"This I will do, yes. Thank you." She slipped the card behind the elastic of her bikini bottom, among 10s and 20s.

As they left the cubicle, North rested his palm on her lower back, where it curved near the tattoo. He removed his hand as they parted and shifted his pants by the belt, deliberately, for the benefit of the bearded men sitting at the table, pretending to watch the stage show. Constable Phillips towered above the bikers, arms folded as if he could hold this position impassively all day. North thought he probably could.

As he approached the table, North winked at Dexter. "Let's get out of here, see what the other strip club owner is up to."

Turk glared at him, once, and looked away. "The other officer that shows up here is a lot more fun than you two."

"What officer's that?"

"A guy we know well. A friend to freedom lovers everywhere."

"Are you trying to tell us something?"

The bikers were keen on the stage show. They couldn't be bothered answering.

### CHAPTER 8

Dexter's Crown Victoria bumped over ice ridges and skidded as he and North exited the parking lot. Dexter steered south onto William Street. Snow crystals twinkled like tiny jewels in the early afternoon sunlight. In his parka, inside the vehicle, North felt a chill pass through him. He turned up the heat, called the station on his cell phone and was patched through to Constable Jennifer Duchamps.

"Beautiful winter day, ain't it boss? Don't you just love this country?"

North's laugh was sardonic. "I'll know once my eyelids unfreeze. We just talked to Candy. She's about as open as a bull's ass in mating season. I might be the same, if I was in her dancing shoes. We're headed over to Friesen's now. Can you get us the exact address and phone number?"

Dexter turned left on Wellington, past the old courthouse. Faded yellow brickwork with a snow-capped roof. A picture postcard of the perfect historical building in winter. Soon to be an empty shell, if the province decided to build a new one instead of bringing the old one up to code.

Constable Duchamps gave him the street address, and North said, "You're a peach, and I've always said so."

"Because of the fuzz on my face?"

"Because you're ripe and juicy and delicious... I've been hanging around Pete the Dutchman too long. Is my old buddy there?"

"One desk away."

"If he's awake, can I talk to him?"

Making elaborate yawning noises, Constable Heemstra came on the telephone. North said, "You get anything from the Campbell fire autopsies?"

"The old guy, Hughie Campbell, died from shots to the chest and head."

"Calibre of bullet?"

"We'll get a definite from ballistics. The doc got one from his right arm, lodged in the bone. Says it's consistent with a 7.90 millimetre. Probably AK-47."

"Jeez, what's that doing in Elgin County?"

"Killing old farmers. Makes no sense to me either."

The Crown Victoria was traveling on black pavement lightened by packed snow and a film of salt. They turned right at the stoplights for First Avenue, Geerlinks Home Hardware on their left, low plazas to their right. North blinked at sunlight hurting his eyes and asked, "And the other deceased?"

"No bullets. Confirmation that he was burned twice, from the burn pattern on his back. It gets weirder. Our John Doe expired from blunt trauma."

"Get out of town."

"I'd love to. This place would make anybody stir-crazy in January. Don't forget my coffee."

"Dex and I are headed over to see if Mr. Abe Friesen is at home. One more thing, have we been investigating biker gang activity, anything like that?"

"The OPP is ongoing, but us? Not since you and Tom Skelding took a shot at it in the summer. You want me to check the files?"

"No, forget I said anything."

As they reached Elm and turned left, the coffee shop tempted North, but that would lead to a cigarette with Dexter. Next stop: half a pack a day. North shut that out of his mind and told Dexter about the autopsy report.

"Maybe that explains the snowmobile tracks," Dexter said. "Somebody gets offed, and somebody doesn't want to involve a funeral director. So they courier our John Doe over hill and dale via snowmobile to bring him to his final resting place in that silo."

North nodded. "Keep it up, and you could make chief some day."

"Now *you're* messing with me."

They spun a right on Holland Ave. with its brick and vinyl-sided twelve-plexes, then left on Aldborough, a 35-year-old residential street of ranches and bungalows. Abe Friesen's driveway had not been shovelled recently. Tire tracks rutted the snow. No vehicle.

On his way to the front door, on an unshovelled path that might have been a sidewalk, North was careful not to slip. No response to the doorbell. The front door was locked. Curtains were drawn across all the windows. "Let's see if he's at work."

Dexter grunted agreement.

Back in the warmth of the unmarked car, North dialled 411 on his cell phone, got the number and called security at the St. Thomas Ford Assembly Plant. He talked to Bud Lancaster, retired from the St. Thomas Police force, who said he would locate Abe Friesen, if the man was working days, and detain him informally at the guard shack.

"I'll tell him I got a late Christmas bonus for him," Bud said.

"Like that's going to happen with all the down weeks those guys had last year."

★

North and Dexter approached the guard shack from doors on opposite sides. Abe Friesen's long blond hair was gathered in a ponytail at the back. He had a flat face with a small nose and big-veined farmer's hands. His black leather jacket was unzipped. He was wearing black jeans with a rodeo belt buckle, tan cowboy boots and a T-shirt whose front displayed a cartoon pin-up girl with gigantic breasts, a crooked, exhausted smile and the line, "I gave her 3 orgasms, and all I got was this lousy T-shirt." A silver amulet hung from a silver chain. He had a diamond stud in his right earlobe.

North said, "Abe Friesen? Or maybe John Travolta after he went shopping at Goodwill?"

Abe looked startled. The officers had both exits covered. He blushed when Dexter said, "Where do you think you're going?"

"Shift change. Time to go home."

North moved in close enough to smell the man's body odour after eight hours on the line. He exaggerated a look of disgust and said, "We were just at your house. Not much going on."

Abe's fair skin flushed from neck to cheeks. He shook his head. His blue eyes studied his running shoes.

North put a hand on Abe's arm. Abe shook him off, and North acted surprised. "You don't want to talk to me? You're much better off with me than my friend Constable Phillips. He'd just love to take out his frustrations on a farm-bred honky like you."

Dexter offered Abe a stone stare. A telephone behind the counter rang and was answered. A delivery woman in a blue uniform rushed through one door, looking for a signature. North said, "We have a few routine questions. Why don't you join us in our vehicle where we have a little privacy?"

Abe looked out the shack window, at cars and trucks streaming from the parking lot. A bald man in a blue cloth coat was selling cheeses from the trunk of an Impala. Abe's face had drained of colour. Spidery lines were showing around his eyes, his mouth. If he looked 28 when they first arrived, he now seemed a decade older. His ponytail waggled as he shook his head. "I already told you people everything."

"We do appreciate that," North said. "And we'd appreciate it even more if we could go over it one more time."

Abe's blue eyes glanced around the small building, as if seeking support for what he would say next. "For the record, I do not leave willingly."

"What kind of useless bullshit is this honky spouting?" North turned to Dexter with a half smile. "He's not going willingly. All we want to do is talk to him. You'd think we were accusing him of..." North stopped on purpose, so he could look back at Abe, who was frightened and pale.

"I can see this isn't easy for you. We understand that." Dexter used a steady voice, as if he were the gentlest of friendly giants. "You're coming off shift, you're thinking of what you're going to do tonight, before the line starts again tomorrow, and you're just another gear grinding away. Same crap, different day. And the police show up. But, see, all we want is to go over things from the night of the fire. We want it, and you need it if you're going to collect insurance."

Abe's shoulders slumped. He exhaled a long breath and nodded once, without saying another word.

Dexter took the driver's seat in the unmarked car sitting in a No Parking zone near the wire fence separating the parking lot from the plant. North held the back passenger door for Abe and closed it after him, then slid into the front. Dexter eased into the parade of vehicles, behind a black F-150 exhausting clouds of steam.

Dexter said, "Word spreads fast in a place like this. People always want to know why the cops pick somebody up. Best thing is to be upfront. Tomorrow, you tell the first three people you see it was routine questions about fire insurance."

"Okay," Abe said. "You ever work in the zoo? That's what I call the place where us animals put in time."

"Places like it. Not this one."

Dexter swung right onto Highway 4, the Talbot Trail, leading to the 401 and after that, London. North and Dexter took turns asking low-key questions. In the front passenger seat, North jotted notes in his small bulky pad. Abe confirmed what the police already had in their reports.

"Here's the tricky part," North said. "Witnesses claim you said somebody was after you."

Dexter jerked his head toward North and said, "The exact words were, 'They told me they would get me.'"

"Thank you," North said. "Doesn't shock me that you would deny you said that, Mr. Friesen. But now that things have settled down, and the police are involved, are you still denying it?"

The man folded his arms together across the front of his leather jacket. His right leg was bobbing so violently the back of his head vibrated. "I did not say that. And I'll contradict any witnesses you dig up."

"You didn't say, 'They told me they would get me?'"

"No."

North let the denial hang in the air for 30 seconds or so before he asked, "What about the people in Saint Tease that night? Your building."

"What about them?"

The Crown Vic slowed as they passed the clover leaf exit to the 401. The wind had picked up, whipping snow across the road. The car shuddered as it encountered each new drift. Doing 40 kilometres an hour, a salt-caked transport truck with Texas plates emerged from the 401, cutting them off.

"We're interested in whether everybody really did escape your fire."

"What are you talking about?"

North looked at Constable Phillips. "Give him that theory, about the mystery man at the second fire."

Dexter accelerated as the Texas truck picked up speed past a set of stoplights. "Two men were found dead at Hughie Campbell's place outside town. One was shot. Interesting thing is the other was burned front and back, but actually died from blunt trauma. Just wasn't his day. You know anything about that?"

"No, course not."

"Makes me wonder whether he might have been killed at your fire." Dexter kept his attention fixed on his driving. "And somebody transported him to the farm."

"You making this up as you go along? Cuz I don't know nothin'."

"There were snowmobile tracks to Hughie Campbell's farm." Dexter's muscular shoulders shifted inside his suit jacket. "Hughie was shot. Why would anybody want to kill a harmless old man?"

"Nobody told me." Abe was attempting to sound cool, but there was a note of desperation in his voice. "So what? Doesn't involve me or my hotel."

"Here's how we work," North interjected to get control of the conversation. "It's pretty rare for something to jump up and grab us by the ass so strong we know we've solved a case, conviction guaranteed. So we focus on what seems most likely, see where that takes us."

"Why all this attention on a law-abiding citizen like me? Are you both nuts?"

"What about your wife?" North asked. "Did she think you were law-abiding? Once you renovated the bar, got into the strip club business, I mean. She a partner in that?"

Abe cranked his head up and blazed one furious look at North before shifting to stare out the front. The afternoon sky was deep blue, lighter at the edges. The sun was reddening in preparation for its disappearing act. The snow in the fields and ditches had been swept by wind into abstract sculptures. White, shading to azure. Abe said, "Everything was legal. I told her that a hundred times, and now I'm telling you."

"But she didn't like it. Is that why she left? Or was it worse than that? She found out you were sampling the merchandise. And what did the Mennonite community think?"

Abe said nothing for a time. When he finally spoke, he was verging on tears. "You can leave my wife, my kids and the Mennonites out of this, thank you very much."

North said, "I thought she was your ex-wife."

"We're still married."

"That's sweet. She must be the forgiving type. Was she also the unresponsive type? Liked it straight up once or twice a month, but otherwise, she's the good mom. Tired all the time, since the kids. Some days, no time to change the kitchen dress. She starts to smell of sour milk and perspiration. Real sex machine, right, Abe?"

"Shut up," Abe's voice was a wail of anger and despair.

"Where's Abe Friesen in all this? Young blond man, strong as bull. Good provider, maybe even a good father to his kids. I understand. I've got two kids of my own. But you have needs, too. It's the twenty-first century. You want some excitement. You buy the old hotel, renovate it while working shifts, get the girls off the circuit. And what started you sampling the merchandise? You get into a little recreational drug use, to set the stage? And where's the harm in that?"

Abe didn't comment, so North continued, "You'd be just the kind of good little bad boy who always wore a raincoat, just in case it started to pour. Scared of bringing something home for those twice-a-month sessions when the mother of your children's in a good mood. Or was that all over for you? Maybe she never did like it. Maybe she pretended, so she could snag a good Mennonite provider like Abe. Once she had her kids, she closed the bedroom door."

"What happened to the routine questions?"

Dexter pulled into the parking lot of a large fruit stand, closed for the winter. North sat in the front seat, waiting. The sun was an enormous coloured ball near the horizon. Abe stared out the side window. Headlights were snaking toward them.

Abe's voice was pleading. "It's none of your business. Whatever went wrong, we are trying to work it out. I care about my kids. No matter what anybody thinks."

"My guess is that's why you don't want to say any more." North kept his tone neutral, as caring as he could make it. "You love your children, and you're afraid something could happen to them."

Abe's answer was filled with anguish. "These people are animals."

Dexter rotated in his seat. "Who are these animals?"

Like a petulant child, Abe twisted his strong body and looked out the other side window at a dark building with shelving for summer fruit.

When Abe didn't say any more for several minutes, Dexter looked back at North, raised dark eyebrows and shrugged. North flung his pen at the dash. "You want to do it this way, that's your call. You think you're doing your kids a huge favour, withholding information. But this isn't some traffic ticket. You could end up with enough charges to make your head spin. Then where will your kids be?"

Abe said, "You have no idea what you're talking about."

North picked up his pen and said through gritted teeth. "Take us back, Constable Phillips. Drop this useless piece of Mennonite garbage off in the parking lot of the Ford plant, see if he can find his car. I'm not sure he could find his own ass in broad daylight, with two hands and a mirror."

Half way to the plant on Highway 4, North turned back to Abe. "I want to apologize for that last comment. I get a little hot-headed sometimes."

"Me too." The blond head in the back seat nodded once. "It's my biggest problem. Me and Dr. Joy Browne, we're working on it."

North kept his voice low and patient. "Listen, if you care that much about your kids, tell us where they are, so we can keep an eye on them."

"Up by the mall."

"Where exactly?"

Abe gave North the address and unit number and said he'd feel better if he knew there was some police protection.

North said nothing.

## CHAPTER 9

The rental units near Elgin Mall were faithful to the design of geared-to-income housing across the province. Narrow, attached building blocks, brick in front. Three storeys including the basement. A small yard out back. A common area with plastic playground equipment glinting under a yard light in front.

Looking like small, awkward Inuit in the dark, children in snow suits and parkas romped among dirty snowbanks. Under a window emitting no light, three shapes huddled over a pile of cardboard, paper and twigs. A lighter sparked. A paper flared and was snuffed by the wind and drifting snow. The figures huddled closer, forming a tighter adolescent shield against the night and the breeze.

The tires crunched ice as the vehicle crept into a Visitors parking spot. North said, "Lighting the Christmas yule log. Teachers must be looking forward to having that crew in the classroom next week."

Dexter said, "Some of us are expected home tonight."

"This won't take long."

"If it does, you call Lynne, explain why I'm working late. We both know how much overtime pay there'll be in this."

"Lynne's a lovely lady. Remind me, again, how a guy like you managed to snag her?"

Dexter exaggerated the flat Native intonation in his voice. "The potency that comes from pure water and elderberry pie. Also hits of Lakota." He grinned and added, "What's your view of Abe Friesen?"

"I think he's lying to us."

A bare bulb illuminated a scuffed front door. A doorbell dangled from strands of copper wires. North removed a glove and banged. A hand-lettered card cellotaped to the door asked: WHERE WILL YOU SPEND ETERNITY? He counted to 30 and hammered again. A woman with an angular face—prominent cheekbones, small chin—answered his knock. A thin child was balanced on one lank hip. An older girl with blue curious eyes peered around the woman's legs, clinging to her mother's slacks with stained fingers.

"Yes?' the woman inquired in a tone that conveyed, "What do you want now?"

"Mrs. Friesen?"

With a free hand, the woman tucked a wandering wisp of thin, reddish blond hair behind her left ear. "You can call me Rachel."

"Can we come in, Rachel? We have a few routine questions."

Fingers that had been fiddling with her hair moved to pick at chapped lips, devoid of make-up. The woman's voice had a lilt, as if she had been raised deep in some half-forgotten rural area. "What kind of questions, like?"

"About your husband. And about the fire, the one at the bar."

Eyes so blue they seemed to have no pupils clouded and darted from one police officer to the other. Her lips curled, and she spoke softly to one side. "The bar's got nothing to do with me. So I got nothing to say."

North kept his tone muted, non-threatening. "Does that mean you're willing to write off your half of the insurance money?"

The eyes widened and stared at North. She shivered and partly closed the door. "Insurance money? I don't have time to follow all that financial mumbo-jumbo. People with husbands, they don't understand how hard it is without one. Well. I understand now, let me tell you."

North shifted his right boot ahead on the threshold, to block closure of the door. "We're letting cold into your home. Why don't we come inside and talk about this?"

The woman's sharp shoulders drooped. She turned with the children, leaving the door open. The officers dropped their boots on a faded turquoise mat in the crowded hall. It was a short walk to a kitchen. Unpacked boxes crowded its walls. Food and plastic bags littered a counter and most of the kitchen table. The tiled floor was missing three squares. A small television set on one of the boxes played *100 Huntley Street*. Rachel Friesen lowered the volume but did not switch it off.

The woman slumped into a chair, plopped the child into the hollow of her lap and pulled a lozenge from an old tin Player's box. "Excuse the mess. We're moving in, and I just can't find the energy."

North and Dexter shifted boxes so they could sit. The woman rubbed her forehead with a palm until the skin reddened and said, "What's this about insurance money?"

North said, "You know about the fire at your husband's club?"

"Some club." The woman laughed and pulled at her nose. "Yeah, I saw the paper, and the neighbours, they all talk."

"When the insurance claim's been settled, you should be entitled to 50 percent."

"You might think that." She turned to Dexter. "What about you? You think there'll be cash for me and the kids?"

Dexter smiled at the woman. "That wouldn't hurt you none, now would it, Rachel?" North noted a change in his intonation, to match the woman's.

Rachel said, "Not at all. Tell me Mr. Strong-Quiet-Type." She released a burst of laughter that sounded borderline hysterical. "Now I don't know nothin' about this, really. But do the cops come investigatin' insurance claims, like? Normally, I mean."

Dexter kept his gaze steady as he said, "We are asked to be involved, in certain circumstances. If there's something amiss."

The woman's eyes narrowed in appreciation of potentially suspicious activities. She jiggled the girl on her lap. The girl's long, blond braid bounced up and down. Her older sister, with the same hairstyle, left the room. The woman said, "There was things goin' on we don't want to think about, never mind discuss with children present. We may be reduced to margarine sandwiches before this is through, but I'm glad we're shed of it, most days. It was an abomination in the sight of the Lord, and we know what happens to people who commit abominations. And do not repent."

North glanced at a calendar on the wall near the humming refrigerator: "Blessed are the meek for they shall inherit the earth."

"You have no idea how hard things can be, without a man." Her jaw tightened and her chapped lips stretched wide until they must have hurt before she pursed them and said, "I never set foot in that place, not while it was in business and not after it was torched."

North said as gently as he could, "You know it was torched?"

The woman laughed manically, her head nodding and nodding. "Oh, yeah. Big time." The child snuggled against the woman's bony chest. Its eyes fluttered in preparation for sleep. A child this unresponsive to the presence of two strange men in the kitchen made North uneasy. At least Maddy and Dylan had made it through the most innocent and vulnerable years; as teenagers, they were developing their own opinions and defenses.

"Is your little girl okay?"

"She's fine, same as always. Not that it's anybody's business but mine." The woman patted the back of the child and then waved a hand in the air. "The whole town knows it, so I'm sure you must have heard. The bikers own the other bar, what's it called? The other one with them strippers. And they wanted to control what my husband called the market. They give him three weeks to shut her down. And when he don't. Well. You see what happened."

"He said all this?" North asked.

The woman's laugh was hollow, echoing. Her jaw muscles bunched as she answered, "I got tired of hearing it. Moaning about this, moaning about that, morning, noon and night. He's tired. He can't keep up the job and the business. This and that. And me saying, so what? Shut down the abomination."

"But he didn't do it."

"The lust got into him, is what I see. Between that and the drugs, he created his own personal perdition."

The child stirred in her lap, but did not cry. The woman's voice maintained its manic pitch. "I refuse to raise my kids among filth like that. So I leave him, even though that's also a sin, to leave the marriage bed, but what else can a person do? Bring that filth and diseases home to the kids? Would you want your children exposed to the AIDS and all that stuff? I can answer that question for you. You would not."

"I can see that was not an easy decision for you, Rachel," Dexter said.

The woman addressed the mess on the table. North would not have been surprised to see black bugs dart, sudden, from beneath a plate. She said, "I'm glad somebody can see it because most people cannot. They put on blinders and will not take them off. Talk, talk, talk behind my back and even some to my face. Women ask me, how could I leave him? Take the children away from their father? Even at church."

North said, "You're still a Mennonite?"

"They shunned us, after Abe went the way he did. Me and the kids, we're with the Pentecostals."

"But the Pentecostals don't agree with your decision to leave the marriage?"

Rachel stared straight ahead. "Even the pastor's wife. What does she know? She's still got her home. Her man is not fornicating with the spawn of the devil."

At last, the woman's tone diminished. "Well. It is a sin when a person does not forgive, but I cannot. That's up to Jesus now."

North thought, and who will forgive me for what I've done to Connie? A long whistle sounded outside. North looked out a small kitchen window. A bang was followed by a spiralling burst of pink sparkles. A trail of smoke descended against the glow of a single streetlight showing through a dingy pane.

"Them kids," said Rachel, shaking her head and speaking calmly, methodically. "You tell them and tell them."

"Are you willing to testify?" North asked. "About what was happening between your husband and the spawn of the devil? I understand how you must feel, and I'm sure a jury would too."

"I do not care about the insurance. I want no dollars that are in any way associated with that place or them girls or drugs. Are we clear on that?"

North heard a sing-song voice in the next room: "Jesus loves me, this I know." North said, "We're clear. So you are willing to testify?"

She was rubbing her forehead again, reaching for another lozenge as she balanced the child. "I'm not big on the courts. But I might be willing to make some kind of statement."

North started to say something, and she cut him off. "Does a person get money for that? I can't do nothing to jeopardize the welfare cheques I got coming. Or the child support to which I am definitely entitled. And I see on the TV where a wife can't testify against her own husband."

"We can't force anyone to testify against anybody else." North con-tinued to keep his voice even. "And there's always doubt about the state-ment of one spouse against another. But in Canada, you're free to take the stand. What difference does it make, now that you're separated?"

"None in the eyes of man. But in the eyes of the Lord, we are still man and wife. The Abe I married was not a man to do the things he got into, believe you me."

The absent sing-song voice was repeating itself: "Yes, Jesus loves me. Yes, Jesus loves me." After listening for a time, North asked, "I thought you and Abe had three children?"

"The oldest one, he's in the common area with the others. Dollars to donuts, he's with the firecracker gang. A strong desire to fire up this and that."

Dexter said, "It's worth keeping an eye on."

"I'm worried he'll go the way of his father. Who would've thought a Mennonite would turn so bad? I heard about this kind of thing when I was a kid, but you never think it will happen to you."

### CHAPTER 10

On the drive back to the station, Dexter asked North, "Anything change for you, now that you've met Mrs. Friesen?"

North peered out at yellow streetlights and passing cars, their lights muted by creeping whorls of white frost on his side window. "Might explain why Mr. Friesen was playing with other people's toys. What did you think?"

"The same. A statement from her might help us pry information out of others. But the Crown couldn't put her on the stand. Can you imagine what would happen under cross examination?"

"She'd fold." North put Southern in his voice. "Like a cheap suit in Vegas." And then some Down East. "She'd crumble like a dried-up leaf, me boy."

North pulled out his cell phone and pushed buttons. "Three calls from the same number. My reputation must have preceded me among the women of this city. And here I thought I'd already nailed all the beauties."

He waited until Dexter had dropped him off at Grand Central apartments, waited until he was inside his own two-bedroom unit, and waited a while longer. He burned one side of a grilled cheese sandwich and ate it anyway. He spent five minutes flipping through the *St. Thomas Times-Journal*. He had a shower and dressed in jeans and a sweater and slippers. He was half way through his second Blue Light before he dialled the number left on his cell. He used the black telephone on an end table by the couch in the living room.

"Is this your cell?" he asked.

"The shit, she is deep," Candy said.

"What happened?"

"You, I must see."

"All right. Where are you?"

"I come to you."

North recited the address for Grand Central—she said she knew the apartments—and his unit number. "Ring me from the lobby."

While he put away cereal boxes and empties and bread bags and groceries scattered across the dining room table and the kitchen counters, North finished his beer. He stacked dirty dishes in the sink. Nothing was the same without Connie. He should have thought of that before engaging in the one-night stand that ultimately drove her away. He shoved various mail and papers, including child support and legal correspondence, into a bureau drawer. "What the hell?" he said out loud before he made the bed and tossed dirty clothes into a bedroom closet. He was checking the refrigerator for wine when the buzzer sounded from the lobby.

Candy wore a full-length brown leather coat with a fluffed-up imitation fur collar, off-white. Her boots had stiletto heels and were the same colour as her coat. She had on a leopard print scarf. No gloves. A lot of make-up. She seemed to be trying to look more like a business woman than a stripper. The effect was spoiled by a shiner around her left eye, a split in her lower lip and swelling in the upper.

"Glad I went to the trouble of making the bed," North murmured to the squeak of the hall closet door as he opened it.

"Pardon, what you say?"

North asked, "Can I take your coat and bags?" and "What happened to you?" almost as one question. She said yes and handed him her satchel, coat and scarf. Under the coat, she was wearing a black mini-skirt and a black top with rhinestones, as if returning from a post-New Year's Eve party. Her purse had vertical stripes, wide and vibrant. She placed it on a stand near North's unopened mail.

She seemed hesitant to enter the living room. But when North indicated the couch with a sweeping gesture of his left arm, she tiptoed in wearing her boots and sat with head bowed. Her long legs in black-tinged pantyhose were pressed tightly together. Her tongue sought and found the wound on her lower lip, gliding over it as she asked, "Something to drink?"

"I have beer and wine."

"No vodka?"

"Sorry."

She wrinkled her nose at him and said, "Okay, wine."

He asked if white was okay. She said white was the best. He delayed asking her more until he had poured a glass for each of them and had said "Cheers."

She answered "Na zdravie" with a weak smile and added, "In English, means 'best health,' some word like that."

He took a seat in a cloth easy chair and sipped his wine. "How is your health?"

"Fine." This was followed by, "Not so good."

"So which is it?'

"Maybe not so good."

"What happened?"

"I am not hit by bus."

North straightened in the chair and looked at the picture of the Canadian winter scene above the couch. That print and a bas relief of an African head in the bedroom had been left by previous tenants. "I wasn't implying you were struck by some form of public transportation."

"These mens, they are trouble."

"I probably know the answer, but which men are these?"

"Turk and Studs."

Silver hoop earrings showed around her hair. North thought about how much of the woman he'd seen at the bar and how little he knew her. "And they decided to lay a beating on you, these two men?"

"Yes."

"You know why?"

"Is because I am talk to you." Candy squirmed on the couch and looked out glass patio doors, at white swirling around a cold balcony.

"But you didn't tell me anything."

"I know this, but..."

When she didn't continue, North said, "All right, I'll bite. But what?"

"They think I am traitor. Send me back."

"And you do not want to go back."

"Like Russian mafia, these mens. Iron fist in glove." She smashed her clenched right hand into her left palm.

"Here, we have due process, rule of law."

Candy shrugged her shoulders and shivered. Her puppy-dog eyes seemed to be asking North a question he wished he could answer. He shook his head once, to break from these thoughts, and said in a quiet voice with no trace of sarcasm. "You called me. What can I do for you?"

"Help."

"We could charge them with assault. Did anyone else see them do this?"

"You are kidding, no?"

"See, that's going to be a problem. No witnesses, it's your word against theirs. And your chosen profession leaves a few strikes against you."

"Should make no difference."

"Assault charges in this country are weird. Sometimes you get a sentence about as long as murder. Other times, they slap wrists, especially with no weapons involved."

The woman's large, unblinking eyes stared at North. She swallowed and said nothing. She had the most perfect neck—muscled and gently curving—that North had seen in a long, long time. A silver necklace looped above the hollow at its base.

Candy crossed one leg over the other. The static rustling of pantyhose on pantyhose. She continued to look at him. Her damaged lips were slightly parted. She sipped from her glass, dribbled some wine and wiped her hurt mouth with the back of her hand. "No police."

"Technically, I am the police."

"I need escape. Get away. I think about this long time, but how? I am not young girl and how long is this life? Not long. You mens, you want young girl to dance."

North drained his glass, pulled himself out of the chair and poured again from the bottle on the table. He waved the bottle toward Candy who nodded. He gurgled wine into her glass, set the bottle on a coffee table and joined her on the couch. She moved her left hand to his right thigh and said, "Help me, please."

"That could be the mistake of a lifetime," North said quietly. "What is it with me and women?"

"What does this mean?" An index finger traced a pattern on his denim.

"I am enough of a fool to say I might help you." His left hand seemed to lift on its own. It brushed a strand of blond hair away from her face.

She grasped this hand and held the palm to her cheek. "I thank you and ask again. What does this mean, this help?"

"You fear these men and want to get away?" *You fear these men*, God, he was starting to talk like her.

"Yes."

"I need some time to work out what I can do for you. So, stay here for a while."

"This apartment, here I can stay?"

"There's an extra bedroom. Did you bring a car?"

She shook her head and asked, "You maybe have something to eat?"

He managed to not burn a grilled cheese sandwich. She wolfed it down, and he made her a second which she ate more slowly, finishing with a smile that seemed to hurt before she swallowed the last of the wine in her glass.

"Another drink?"

"Thank you very much, no." She slumped backward in her chair, patted her belly and said, "Is good. I do not know I am this hungry."

"What did you bring with you?"

"A little toilet. Costume and, m-m-m-m, nightclothes."

North showered and shaved in a state of anticipation. When he emerged from the bathroom, the smell of marijuana was strong. A haze hovered near the ceiling. North made no comment.

In his beige bathrobe and slippers, he showed Candy the location of towels and the spare bedroom. He returned to his own room and listened to the running of water. Occasional splashing. The spiralling suck as the bathtub emptied. Mild bumping. When she finished, would she join him in his room? Part of him rejected the idea. He was recently separated, it would mean nothing to her. Nothing. Forget it. It was what she did for a living. Other parts of him throbbed with hope and longing.

The bathroom door thumped. The spare bedroom door opened. He rolled over. Should he go to her? Was she waiting for him, wanting her man with the beautiful eye to bring her comfort and, perhaps, ecstasy? He wouldn't be like the others who did things to her for gratification and power and money.

Half an hour passed. North slipped into a dream. A model, with a single Cyclops eye, dressed in a red negligee, danced for him, abandoned him, and gyrated in front of Pete Heemstra in a smoke-filled bar. He asked for a cigarette, and Pete turned him down. He drew his piece, had it trained on a target on Pete's back when he woke up, disturbed, restless, heart pounding. He turned on a bedside lamp and picked up a book about Alexander the Great.

Fifteen minutes later, he heard a gentle rapping on his bedroom door. "Yes?" he said.

"Please, may I enter?"

"Just a minute."

He switched off the lamp, half sat up and smoothed the bed coverings. He lay back down, rolled over so he was facing the door, his hands between his thighs and said, "Come in."

She opened the door. "Why light is off?"

North straightened his legs, shunted to his back, pulled covers up to his chin and said, "I don't know." He sat up and switched on a lamp with a wide, pink oval base and a frilled top. Left over from a previous life.

"Sit down." North patted the edge of the bed.

A noise. The mattress dented. She was turned away from him. Her hair reached the bumpy curve of vertebrae beneath a red negligee.

He shouldered himself in her direction and placed a hand on the long muscles to the right of her neck. She didn't respond to this or reject his touch. His fingers began to massage the tightness. He looked at the African bas relief on the wall above her head—he thought of it as his little black dude picture—and said, "You're tense. Couldn't you sleep?"

She shook her head, no, turned toward him and caressed his cheek with her palm. "You are good man, no?"

North manoeuvred himself a few inches left and again onto his back. "My reputation as a saint obviously preceded me. But I'm afraid you've mistaken me for someone who gives a shit."

Her nails were slivers of steel brushing his cheek. He shivered and touched her wounded lips with his own fingers. "You couldn't sleep?"

She swung her head. The sweep of her hair was as graceful as the motion of a ballerina on stage or a figure skater on ice. He said very quietly, almost a whisper, "Do you want to talk?" He was conscious of his own breath, of its sour taste after his short sleep. If this headed anywhere, he should get up and brush his teeth.

"What is to say? No sleep, not yet."

North shifted his left hand to her left shoulder and his right hand to the black button on the lamp. The room went dark. Candy became a shape, defined by the dull glow of light emanating from the city between the parted curtains. He made room for her and she rolled soft into him under the covers. "Hold me," she whispered.

He held her.


## CHAPTER 11


At 4:13 a.m. according to the red letters on his bedside clock radio, North woke with a slight headache, a dry throat, an erection, and Candy's arm across his abdomen. He considered what to do, eased himself from under the woman's arm and tiptoed to the bathroom to scoop handfuls of water into his mouth. This eased his headache and soothed his dehydrated larynx and tongue. He surveyed himself in the mirror—a less-than-tall, slightly gangly man with a small paunch, no matter how hard he exercised—and wondered what his diminishing erection was telling him. "That you're a complete idiot," he said to his unruly hair.

Candy had rolled to the other side of the bed. If her even breathing were to be believed, she was enjoying the deep sleep of an exhausted person with a clear conscience. North wanted to read from a bedside novel. But he had no desire to risk waking her so he eased himself under the covers as quietly as he could and thought about a Mennonite man who was into drugs and strippers, about the man's peculiar wife. His mind shifted back, circling and spinning, to two dead men in a farmhouse fire, the bitterness of that wintry night, the emergency services personnel in attendance, the condition of the bodies. In an attempt to stop this circus in his head, he fixed his eyes on the yellowish glow of street lighting oozing between the parted bedroom curtains. He repeated the Lord's Prayer to himself, a mantra that sometimes worked.

North woke again at 5:45 a.m. The same woman was in the same bed with him. He had a different erection. He slipped out of bed and into his bathrobe, found his slippers and padded to the narrow galley kitchen to make coffee in a drip machine. All this activity looked after his morning arousal. About 15 minutes later, he heard stirring noises in the bedroom, and his heart rate increased a notch. The commotion moved to the bathroom where water ran intermittently. North considered how this might go, a morning after that wasn't a morning after.

Candy had reapplied make-up, but her face was lined, her eyes streaked with pink. She had found one of North's old green bathrobes, a ratty one that, if it weren't so comfortable, he would have already donated to the Salvation Army. She said "Good morning" and slumped on the couch instead of joining him at the table. The whites and greys and greens of the Canadian winter scene above the sofa were especially depressing today.

"Coffee?" North waved his mug toward her.

"Coffee," she said. "Yes."

"Cream? Sugar?"

"I like my coffee and my mens strong and black." Her smile looked insincere.

In the cupboard, he found a dark blue mug imprinted with "Ford St. Thomas Assembly Plant." It looked clean. He wiped lingering dust out of it with a towel, poured her a cup and carried it into the living room. He warmed up his own coffee in the kitchen and brought it to his easy chair. "How are you this morning?"

Candy frowned and gave him one wild look before her eyes veered to the low coffee table. Metallic sleeves protected the bottoms of its thin round legs. She sipped from her cup and reached into the pocket of his old housecoat. She extracted a hand-rolled cigarette and a white lighter. She lit it, inhaled deeply, holding in the smoke as she leaned across to offer him the joint and a view of more breast than he was accustomed to seeing in his apartment before eight in the morning. Or any time of the day. "You want some?" Her voice sounded both muffled and harsh.

A pungent smell pervaded the apartment. North said, "A little early for me. How much dope did you smuggle into my place?"

Candy seemed to relax as she took another long drag and held it. "A little. Never early for me."

"Where did you get it?"

Candy rolled her shoulders, casually, indifferently. "Is mine. Is how they pay, is part."

"They pay you with weed?"

"Yes, is part. The tip, we keep. And the drug, they have much. They, m-m-m-m-m, they control. They desire the market."

"We have trouble nailing them for it," North said. "Maybe you can be a witness for the Crown."

Candy shrugged her shoulders, smiled, and her hand moved to her mouth. Smiling seemed to hurt. "Like on the TV. Maybe."

"Yeah and maybe that's all we need on the witness stand. A stripper who smokes a joint so she can face the day."

"Be nice man." She tried a frown, failed to maintain it, and the smile returned. She licked a lip that seemed less swollen this morning. "You are not nice man."

North said, "Just for the record—and I know how complicated this is, given our current approach to marijuana laws—but you really shouldn't be smoking up in a sergeant's apartment."

Candy lowered her eyelids and wriggled inside the robe, a slow-motion parody of what she did for a living. "Come on, you big guy. Is time to loosen up."

The curtains to the concrete balcony were drawn. Dawn was beginning to seep around the edges. He should prepare for work. "This is about as loose as I get. If I really go nuts, I'll ask you for a regular cigarette."

"You mens, I know what you want." She patted the worn green fabric of the sofa cushion beside her. "Come, sit close by Candy."

For a few seconds, North's entire body wanted to do that. He had not had sex since Connie left, but last night had awakened him. Candy was stoned, she was wounded, he could take advantage. Later, he might or might not regret it. He closed his eyes and shook his head, clearing it. "You're too tall for me. It would never work."

"Okay. You snooze, you lose." She finished the joint with deep satisfaction and ground out the glowing butt in a brown and orange ceramic ashtray. Her eyes glazed. She slumped back on the couch, the robe open, her legs parting. She closed her knees, shifted them onto the couch, rolled toward him, twitched a small smile at him and crossed her arms over her breasts.

"You get high every morning?"

Candy nodded contentedly. She moved her left arm and bent forward. The robe opened, exposing a nipple. "Every day is best way."

North finished his coffee and considered Ms. Ivana Genska of Mississauga, also known as Candy. What he might do to her. What she needed. How a statement from her could help the investigation. "Time to get ready for work. Me, I mean."

Candy lazily moved her head up and down in the affirmative. She slid his robe over her exposed breast and didn't reply.

"I think you should stay here." North coughed and cleared his throat. "It seems safer than anything else I can think of. And you may be able to help us a lot, in return. I'll leave you a spare key in case you need to go out. And don't let anybody in. And I mean, nobody."

Her head bobbed in agreement. "No. Body."

"I'll check on you from time to time. There's bread and soup and cereal. Tomatoes in the fridge. You won't starve."

"I am big girl. Thank you." She smiled at him. "You are good man to do this. Be careful at your work."

"I always am."

Her eyes were closing. "They have people on police, is what they say."

North was instantly alert. His voice was louder, sharper. "They have someone on the inside?"

Candy nodded. "Is what I hear."

"Who is it?"

She shook her head. "Only talk. I never see this man."

"Man, I hope you are wrong. You sure you don't know his name?"

"No, but you see? Is why I say, take care."

CHAPTER 12

North was at his desk by 7:45. A pink note, balanced on top of a stack of files, said Henry Shaw wanted him to call. North ignored this for the moment. Chief Kenneth MacArthur had sent an email to all staff about a meeting at eight o'clock. The chief usually met with department heads at nine.

On the way to grab a coffee before the meeting, he asked Pete, "What's with the chief sending everybody emails? You get caught with your fingers in the cookie jar?"

"Worse. Quarters from the pop machine. It's my float, next time we go to the casino."

North's mind flashed to one of his favourite pastimes. "No time these days."

At two minutes to eight, Inspector Archibald "Baldy" Simpson barked for attention. The sea of black uniforms, and a few plain clothes, straightened, obeyed. Chief MacArthur—his hair grey, his bearing erect—strode into the room. Simpson's voice snapped again, "At ease," and officers relaxed into chairs.

Shorter than Simpson and lacking his vocal pipes, MacArthur used determination and a very direct gaze to command respect. North was happiest when those eyes homed in on someone or something other than him.

In precise tones, scanning his audience as he spoke, MacArthur said, "This is a sad day for the St. Thomas Police Service. I have the unpleasant duty to inform you that Constable Tom Skelding has been suspended with pay. Allegations are being investigated by the Ontario Provincial Police from outside Elgin."

If it were possible to hear a collective gasp, North thought he had just detected one—as if the officers in the room had breathed in, held and released the same breath. This was followed by low-level rumbling and whispering. North was immediately concerned about Tom. How was this possible?

Simpson called the officers to order.

Chief MacArthur continued, "Constable Skelding is alleged to have been in possession of crack cocaine. We will not be revealing this to the press at this time. No release will be made until charges, if any, are laid.

"We know him, we know his wife, we know his family. There will be a tendency to believe this can't be true. And perhaps it isn't. That's why I've requested the OPP to investigate."

The chief unfurled a sheet of paper that had been rolled in his strong right fist and glanced at it. "I expect you to treat this with the utmost respect. The rumour mill in this town is fast and vicious. You will tell people the truth if asked—and only if asked. Any officer going beyond that will deal personally with me. If you were Constable Skelding, you would expect the same. Do I make myself perfectly clear?"

As one, the officers sat tall in their chairs and barked, "Yes, Sir."

★

The chief left. Inspector Simpson dealt with other morning items, including updates on the deaths at the Campbell farm. Few people seemed to be listening. When this ended, North commiserated with officers expressing shock, questions and dismay. After about five minutes of this, he approached Inspector Simpson and asked, "Two minutes in your office?"

Simpson said, "Meeting with the chief starts in 10. Does it have to be now?"

"I think so."

Inspector Simpson led the way and closed his door. He moved a stack of reports from his desk to the floor, glanced at a telephone message and waved a large hand, "Have a seat. From my experience, two minutes is never two minutes. Let's keep it as close as we can."

"Yes, Sir."

"You have my full attention."

North cleared his throat and looked at the desk before directing his gaze up to meet the inspector's eyes. "I have been in communication with the woman who gave us the heads-up on Abe Friesen the night of the fire at Saint Tease. The one who claimed somebody was out to get Friesen."

"I recall the allegation."

"This woman has been mistreated by some of the Pythons who own the other club in town. This mistreatment has encouraged her to begin to talk. This morning, she told me the bikers say they have somebody inside the police force."

Inspector Simpson straightened in his chair and smoothed his hands over hair, combed in a 1950s wave. "How credible is this woman?"

"Reasonably, I'd say." North raised his eyebrows and spread his hands. "But she's a stripper."

Simpson's bright eyes were alert and searching as he stood, paced across the floor to a beige filing cabinet, leaned an elbow across the top of it, looked at North, looked away, and returned to his seat. "Thanks for bringing it to my attention. It could be anyone on the force."

The inspector picked up a ballpoint pen, hurled it, end-over-end, toward the filing cabinet. The pen smashed against a corner of the cabinet and fell, cracked, to the floor, where he left it. His voice was harsh and lacked its usual precision. "I hate this."

"Yes, Sir, we all do. Not that we know Skelding is guilty of anything."

"No, but we're pretty sure about the cocaine." The man's round, darkened eyes were fierce. North was glad he wasn't the one under suspicion.

The inspector placed both elbows on the desk. He closed his eyes briefly, and when he opened them, some of the fury was spent. He straightened his back and left his chair. He walked over to pick up the pen and flip it into a wastebasket under his desk before sitting again. "You haven't told anyone about this?"

North considered this question briefly, just to be sure, before saying, "No, Sir."

"You will tell no-one. As of this moment, only you and I are privy to this information. So if I hear it on the rumour mill, I'll know who let it out." His next sentence was enunciated clearly, with spaces between certain words. "And it sure as hell... will not... be me."

"I understand, Sir."

The eyes had returned to their normal brightness when they focused back on North. "What were you doing with a stripper before the staff meeting this morning?"

North shifted in his seat and attempted a deadpan expression. "Checking my sources. She was on the list."

Simpson raised bushy eyebrows. He pursed his lips. His telephone sounded. He took the call, didn't say much into the receiver, other than that he was aware of something, and he'd be right there. When he finished, he turned back to North. He seemed distracted. "To summarize, I'll keep what you said under advisement. Nothing panics police officers faster than the idea that one of their own is a Judas. Now go to work. I'm late for a meeting."

## CHAPTER 13

Some time before North's arrival in St. Thomas, the Police Services Board had authorized the purchase of new, smaller furniture so officers and staff could more easily squeeze into incredibly tight quarters. North's difficulty keeping his paperwork under control added to the feeling he was working in a cluttered version of Peewee's Playhouse. His St. Thomas superiors had issued him three memos about his messy desk in the six months he'd been sergeant. Those memos were around somewhere. North found his telephone and called Henry Shaw.

Henry's answer was a wheezy, "Shaw here."

"Carl North. You asked me to give you a call."

Henry spoke like a man trying to conserve every available ounce of oxygen. "I want to show you something. Can you meet me at Saint Tease?"

"Sure." The filing could wait. That was the thing about paperwork—it never went anywhere. "Are we talking right away?"

Henry coughed and said, "Could be at the site in five or 10 minutes."

★

"Not much left, is there?" North was looking west, at a cracked concrete foundation. The open basement was filled with charred wood, twisted metal, and appliance remains. The exterior foundation walls were concrete, the interior ones made of two layers of brick. Somebody had laid two-by-12 planks over these walls. Snow had drifted in, making a black and white mess. A sign for Saint Tease rose 18 feet high near the road. Its brilliant yellow plastic promoted "Girlz, Girlz, Girlz."

Henry grinned, took a shallow breath and said, "Not too sexy now, is it?" He coughed, and his coughing morphed into wet choking. He spat, inhaled as deeply as he could and said, "Son of a bitch."

"You sure you should be out here? It's gotta be 20 below."

Henry's thin frame seemed bulkier in his winter coat. He shrugged and said, "There's something you should see." The man approached the foundation and stepped up to one of the planks. Although he was nervous, North followed. His extreme fear of heights kicked in, over something as minor as crossing planks above a basement when he had nothing solid to grasp with his hands.

As he reached the middle of the building, Henry stopped and pointed at two brick walls in succession. "That room was below the kitchen, and this room was below the laundry. It's the laundry that interests me the most."

Henry coughed gently as he descended an aluminum ladder. North teetered above this ladder and felt relief as soon as his gloved hands were on the top, his feet on rungs. When North reached the bottom, Henry said, "Warmer down here. Out of the breeze."

North nodded. The burned wood and detritus odour couldn't be good for Henry's lungs.

"I was studying what's left of these appliances." Henry gestured toward two gutted dryers and one washer that had fallen from above.

"Not much to go on."

"Every fire tells a story. This one was much hotter than the Campbell fire. The natural gas mixture must have been very close to its upper explosion limit. We got complete combustion, not one of those big explosions that bounces the roof off, and everything settles back down from there." This was a long speech for Henry. His choking cough returned. He found a clear lozenge in his pocket and wiped at his watering eyes. "Sorry," he said, as he sucked on the candy.

"These old frame buildings make great tinder."

"About a hundred years old. Very solid foundation with the concrete exterior and the brick walls down here. Look at this dryer." Stepping over debris, Henry moved toward the appliance.

"Okay."

"The natural gas pipe. The connector is gone. There's a clean break, or I should say, no break at all. The threads are intact."

"Which means?"

"With this dryer, the line's not here. On this other one, it's still attached. That's why it's hanging half way down the wall."

"So you're saying what? The natural gas line to one dryer was unscrewed?"

"Sure looks like."

"And that means what?"

"I checked with the owner. The building had been empty five years when he bought it. It had been a bar before it became Saint Tease. You remember? It was called The Old Ninety-Seven, no, course you wouldn't know that. You're too new here. Anyway, 25 years before that, it was a regular hotel with overnight guests." Henry unwrapped a second lozenge and surveyed the basement room.

"Help me out here, Henry."

"The laundry facilities haven't been used for years. But the appliances were still there, natural gas lines in place with the gas shut off."

"Which means...?"

"Saint Tease was using the kitchen for food service. Hamburgs or fries and such. They had natural gas stoves, over there." With a glove, Henry indicated a soot-covered brick wall. "I think some clever bastard knew there was still gas to these appliances. Sneaked in here. Unscrewed the line to the dryer. Natural gas rises, lighter than air."

Henry paused and took several short breaths sucking on his candy before his breathing seemed to be controlled. "You'd have 30 minutes to an hour. Lots of time before the gas would fill this room, travel across the hall and settle down to the level of the pilot light on a stove in the kitchen. You get ignition on a nice gas-fuelled fire."

"All that from a pipe, eh, Henry?"

"All that from a pipe."

"Why would somebody do that?"

"That's your department. Other than fooling around, or because some bastard likes it too much, the two most common motives for arson are greed and revenge. Could be either, but in this case, I like revenge."

North looked at the thin, pale man and smiled. "Maybe somebody else did, too."

## CHAPTER 14

North took a call at his desk at 11:05 a.m. Two minutes into the conversation, he wished he were back writing boring reports for the day clerk to keyboard.

Later, he would check the number he had scribbled down from call display. It originated from a pay phone in Shedden. Not much to go on, although the Pythons' clubhouse was in a farmhouse west of that town. The voice sounded deep and well aged by years of smoking and drinking. "What the fuck you doing with that girl?"

Playing dumb, North asked, "What girl?"

"The girl you're hosing in your apartment. You want to do her, I can understand that. But why'd you keep her overnight?"

The speaking pattern seemed familiar. North asked, "Who's calling?"

"The tooth fairy." A definite lisp. "I done her a time or two myself. Outstanding, man. Really outstanding."

Deep within himself, North tightened up. "What's this about?"

"Mamma likes the rough stuff, you notice that? Takes to it like a baby takes her mommy's tit."

Pressure rose steadily from North's abdomen to his chest and with it, anger that he tried to control. He coughed to clear his throat and took a sip of coffee from a cold, white ceramic cup emblazoned with the insignia of the RCMP. He said in what he hoped was a disinterested tone, "Could I have your full name and address?"

"See, here's how this goes." The man's deep laugh grated in North's ears, and suddenly he knew who it was. "You head back to your apartment for dinner or supper, whenever you get there. And you come up—bang—

face-to-face against one of those situations, where you got to ask, what do I do here? And either way, it's you who ends up being the sick fuck responsible."

North straightened in his chair.

"That piece of eye candy you been messing with. It wasn't as if she wasn't warned. And buddy boy, there's a message in all this for you."

Click.

Hum.

North replaced the receiver. Outside his small office, plain clothes and uniforms—his buddies, his compadres, people who outranked him and people he outranked, spit and polished and ready to roll—went about their daily business with telephones and files and paperwork leading to endless computer work and trails of correspondence. They joked, they communicated, they jockeyed for position. They opened files or closed them or advanced them one more crucial step. Often it was a small step. But when it was there, it was celebrated. North understood it all.

But at the moment, he couldn't talk to any of them. Not his superiors or his inferiors or those of the same rank. He couldn't go into the call he'd just taken without introducing the topic of a stripper, potentially a witness in a murder investigation, who had slept in his bed the night before. And what exactly was she doing in his apartment?

North called the front desk and said he was heading out for lunch. He exited by the side door to the parking lot. Snow streamed across white and blue vehicles. He started an unmarked Crown Vic, cranked the heat and fan on high, left his seat to brush off the windshield and re-entered the vehicle.

He drove past a snow-dusted bronze statue of a nude mother and son in front of the concrete and glass library. He turned left, went up a block, and right onto Talbot by the stoplights. Seven mental health clients, looking like refugees from a Siberian prison, were on the icy sidewalk, smoking and pacing and talking.

He accelerated, spinning his wheels, onto the main drag. Dirty snow had been piled high along sidewalks. Passageways had been scooped through them in the hope that shoppers would abandon vehicles at various angles and venture indoors. Left at the lights on Queen and left into the parking lot for Grand Central apartments.

Lines of snow eddied from pale grey skies. The faded yellow-brick building—twelve storeys high in two towers—could have been an apartment complex in any city in the world. Blue graffiti was spraypainted above a delivery door. North drew the collar of his parka up around his neck and hunkered his shoulders forward. Head lowered against the gale, he approached the entrance.

The lobby had a mirrored wall and mailboxes and welcoming furniture. Except for one thin, white-haired woman in a long grey cloth coat, wool toque and white running shoes, it was vacant. The woman used small leapfrogging motions to advance her walker toward glass exit doors. The elevator seemed slow. A smell like sauerkraut, but more acrid, rose from the moisture, dirt, salt and snow tramped into the carpet.

The hallway to his apartment was empty.

North inserted a key into the lock of his door.

The interior of the apartment was quiet. North felt a chill.

"Candy?" His keys tinkled as they hit a stand holding a lamp and some unopened bills he should have at least scanned in recent days. No purse beside the mail. A lamp on the stand was the sole light source, casting the apartment in shades of black and grey. The drapes to the balcony were closed.

"Candy, you here?"

North switched on an overhead hall light and slid open a closet door. He thought, as he had a dozen times before, that he really must see if he had some WD-40 to take care of its squeak. As he took out a bulky hanger for his parka, he spotted the long brown leather coat with the imitation fur collar hanging from the rod. Draped over the hook of the hanger was a leopard print scarf.

"Fuck," he said quietly. "Fuck, fuck, fuck."

His mind skipped to the telephone call that had brought him here. He reviewed the conversation and got no further. He hooked his parka beside the brown coat. Bending over, he untied his black boots and slipped his feet out of them. Sock feet would be better for the tiled areas in the kitchen and bathroom.

North listened. His ears picked up mechanical heating noises from the building and movement in the outside hallway.

He rubbed his arms. Why was it so cold in here?

He flicked on a light in the galley kitchen. A coffee odour. A dinner knife with traces of margarine lay beside a toast remnant. The drip coffee maker was off. He felt the pot. Room temperature.

He checked the bedroom. His queen-sized bed had been made. Neatly, by Candy, he assumed. He was impressed by this domestic gesture. He walked quickly around the bed, peered under it, opened the closet door, gave his clothing a cursory glance, saw nothing unusual.

The spare bedroom was even neater. Candy's brown satchel, the one he had placed in the hall closet when she had arrived, was leaning against the side of a white cupboard. No purse in sight. A make-up bag and hair brush were aligned beside each other on a white bedside table. The bed had been as carefully made as his own.

The dining room and living room seemed exactly the same and exactly as ordinary as when he had left them earlier in the day. He switched on a couch-side lamp and studied the thermostat. It read 17 degrees Celsius. It was set for 23. He turned it to 25, slumped into his easy chair and thought about what Candy had left in the apartment, about what seemed to be missing, and about the telephone call. Turk, he was sure it was Turk, had said North would find something when he came home for dinner or supper. North would have to make up his mind. And one way or another, he would be responsible. What the hell did that mean?

Most of what Ivana Genska, a.k.a. Candy had brought to the apartment was still here. Where was Candy and why was her black purse missing? Maybe she'd gone for some air. Not without her coat, in this weather. Perhaps some exercise within the building? The ground floor housed offices and a convenience store. She could have grabbed her purse and gone for cigarettes.

What was causing his apartment to cool down? His gaze shifted to the heavy beige curtains covering the glass patio doors leading to his concrete balcony. The curtains swayed. Had Candy left the patio doors ajar?

He walked softly across the room and swung the curtains wide.

The glass patio door was open a crack. On the balcony, exposed to slanting streaks of white, wearing North's old housecoat and nothing else, was Candy.

She was leaning back on a plastic white lawn chair. It was one of two North had stored out here when he'd moved into the apartment. Her hands and her face were tinged with blue. Her eyelids flicked open, blinking against snow pellets. Her eyes seemed enormous. Her damaged mouth had been sealed shut with a strip of grey duct tape. Tape circled her wrists and ankles, securing the woman to the plastic chair.

North's right hand found a handle part way up the glass patio door. Candy shook her head, her jaw muscles bunching, as if she were trying to scream inside the duct tape. Nothing came out.

North whipped the patio door sideways. And immediately recognized his mistake.

The chair had been set on the edge of the balcony, with one rear leg teetering over the concrete. Somehow, by opening the patio door, North had sent the chair further out. There was nothing to stop it. The chair came up against snow and wind. Where was the plexi-glass barrier?

A second plastic leg tilted backward over the edge.

The chair swayed in temporary equilibrium.

It tilted further.

Candy's knees spread as the front of the chair lifted. She rolled back with it.

In one frantic motion, North twisted himself away from the curtain and through the door.

He grabbed the slim rope above the snow. Its other end was looped around a front leg of the falling chair. He had it, one end of it. But the rope jerked, burning his clenched bare hand. Candy's weight seemed enormous. The strain was unbearable, tearing at his shoulder. The balcony was slippery. He was off balance. There was nothing to give him purchase. The rope tore through his fist.

The woman performed a slow, helpless plummet from the fifth floor. Whatever rage or terror or confessions were forming inside her, whatever she might be desperately trying to express, none of it could be heard through duct tape.

Her descent seemed to take forever. The chair bounced when it hit, and Candy did not move.

North sank to his knees. Immune to the temperature, his fingers sifted through snow, as if it were wind-swept sand on a beach.

There was no-one near the body.

She must be dead.

North's gaze lifted to the snow-choked roof of the apartment parking garage and the open parking area beside it with its white-covered mounds of vehicles. From there, his eyes shifted to take in an alley and the flat tops of the C & G Tire and *Times-Journal* buildings and beyond them, a city parking lot with a few vehicles, and further on, the Bell building and the parking lot of Holy Angels Church, where a silver SUV was exiting, as if this were an ordinary winter day.

As North straightened, he brushed his hands together. He swept snow off his knees. Cold and dampness penetrated his extremities.

North, fully awake, looked down again at Candy. "Shit," he called out. He slid the patio door shut after him, raced across the living room floor to the telephone on a stand beside the couch and punched in 911. As soon as he'd conveyed the basics, he hung up and called the station. "We need Criminal Investigations. Scenes of Crime people. And ask the staff sergeant to come. Tell him it's a personal favour to me."

His mind began to work. The plexi-glass panel, the one that should have protected Candy, had been removed. It had been set against another plexi-glass panel, still in place. There were boot prints in the eight inches of snow on the balcony. They were clear to him now, as clear as what had transpired. Candy had been duct-taped to the chair and carried out to the balcony. One end of a yellow plastic rope had been tied to a front leg of the chair. The other end, already knotted, had been pulled taut and then anchored by closing the patio door against it. Not closed all the way, left open that crucial little bit. When North had flung the patio door wide, his action had released the chair.

He ran from the apartment, to see what, if anything, he could do for Candy.

## CHAPTER 15

Constables Jennifer Duchamps and Pete Heemstra sat opposite North at his dining room table. North was wearing his parka. With the constant opening and closing of the patio door, his living quarters were freezing. Jennifer began with a good-cop shtick. "Just routine," she assured him with a pleasant smile. "You know the ropes."

North folded his arms in front. "Do you realize how threatening the word 'routine' sounds from this side of the table?"

A frown creased Jennifer's brow, and her cheeks reddened. North ignored Jennifer's discomfort and said, "I really would appreciate it if Vandenberg could join us."

Pete left for a brief chat with Staff Sergeant Norval Vandenberg in the living room. North's superior officer returned with Pete and took a seat beside North. "Are you sure you're ready for this? Without legal representation?"

"Look, I don't consider this my official statement." North spread his hands, palms up in front of him, acting more open to questioning than he felt. "But I wanted you, as my immediate superior, to hear it from the horse's mouth. So I don't look like a horse's ass, later."

"All right, Carl." Pete Heemstra's eyes bored in on North. "But I have to tell you, official or unofficial, you have the right to silence and the right to counsel and all that."

Holding Pete's gaze, North said, "My brain didn't freeze over in the last half hour. Just my balls."

Vandenberg smiled. "What did you want to tell us?"

"Can we put away the notebooks?"

Vandenberg nodded. Pete and Jennifer tucked away books and pens. North spoke quietly so it wouldn't travel all over the room, but he tried to keep his voice even. "I caused Ivana Genska, the stripper also known as Candy, to go over the edge of the balcony. But I didn't do this. Somebody else did."

"You can be impulsive and stubborn." Jennifer used a conciliatory tone. "But nobody here thinks you did this."

"Thank you. And your nose is looking a little brown."

"And you can be a real jerk." Jennifer glanced away, her cheeks colouring again. "We do need to know what she was doing here. And about the marijuana odour in your apartment."

North studied his rather small hands and wondered how clean they really were. He could have been smarter about some things over the last two days. "There's some ground we need to cover."

He reviewed what had happened from the night of the two fires up to the point where Candy had telephoned, asking to meet at his apartment. "Her face was a mess. She'd been beaten by two guys from the Pythons. There were no other witnesses."

A minor commotion arose in the living room. Vandenberg was called away. When he returned, he said, "She's still alive, this Candy who fell."

"What?" North said.

"The emergency medical people say she's alive. She's in bad shape, she's unconscious, but she's breathing."

Relief welled up inside North. He blinked his eyes, against tears. "Thank God. How is that possible?"

"The chair cushioned some of the shock. She landed in snow. And had an angel with her on the way down."

"A snow angel," Jennifer said.

Pete said, "A-w-w-w, that's so cute."

They discussed Candy's fall and the odds against a full recovery.

"She knows things about the Pythons and their attempts to control the local drug trade." North turned to Vandenberg. "Plus there was a matter I spoke to Inspector Simpson about in private."

Vandenberg raised his eyebrows but otherwise offered no expression. "Unless there's a direct connection to today's death, I see no need to go into that at the moment."

North nodded and said, "Somebody called me at work—I suspect it was Turk—making me think I had to get back here."

Jennifer looked around the apartment. "So the knight in shining armour came charging home."

"No signs of forced entry. Candy must have buzzed them up."

Pete continued to stare at North. He found Pete's blue eyes unnerving. "Them? There was more than one?"

"I'm assuming. It's a motorcycle *gang*, Pete."

"Yeah, you are assuming."

"Check the balcony, see how many boot prints you find."

"Trust me, we're doing all that. What did you find when you first got here?"

"It was weird, like somebody was here and not here. The curtains were drawn. Candy's stuff was in the closet and the spare bedroom. I felt a draft and realized the patio door must be open."

Jennifer said, "That's what drew you to the balcony? You wanted to know where the draft was coming from?"

"Exactly. They had duct-taped her to the chair. Candy was half frozen. I thought hypothermia was killing her. So I opened the patio door."

North was surprised by the emotions this roused in him. He didn't trust himself to speak without his voice breaking. He paused and said, "You got a smoke, Pete?"

Pete tossed him a cigarette and leaned over to light it with a black butane lighter. North inhaled deeply, coughed and said, "Thanks." He took a shallower drag, and exhaled. "It's like that crazy *Airplane* movie. I picked the wrong day to quit smoking." He smiled bitterly.

Vandenberg said, "Tell us exactly what happened when you opened the door."

"Somebody had removed a pane of plexi-glass from the balcony. Candy's chair was right at the edge. I couldn't see it in the snow, but they had run a plastic rope from one leg to the bottom of the door. Knotted at the end. They closed the patio door on the knot. That's all that was keeping the chair on the balcony. You'll find yellow cord attached to the chair."

Jennifer watched an officer re-enter the apartment from the balcony. "We're getting photos of everything."

North said, "I flung the door open. That released the rope. The chair shifted, and over it went, backward."

Jennifer's sympathetic eyes were back on North. "You must have felt awful."

North smoked in silence before saying, "It's about two steps from the door to the edge of the balcony. Didn't matter, I grabbed the rope but couldn't hold it." He showed his rope-burned palm.

A siren wailed below. The ambulance was pulling away. Jennifer said, "And you feel terribly guilty about that."

North's cigarette sizzled out in a white mug with half an inch of cold coffee.

Pete's tack was not as sympathetic as Jennifer's. "You think somebody tried to kill her this way, because... ?"

"She was talking to a police officer. They needed to shut her up."

"By they," Pete said, "you mean the Pythons."

"Yeah, and you know what I think? It's up close and personal with these guys."

Pete asked, "Because she worked for them?"

"That, plus it was a kick for them, another high in their miserable little lives."

"This next part is the tough part, you understand?" Pete Heemstra kept his voice level. There was no noticeable change in the sharp Dutch features of his face.

North made sure his own tone was neutral. "Ask away."

"Jennifer hinted at it earlier." Pete's blue eyes remained steady. "This Ivana Genska was here overnight, in your apartment. A stripper with gang connections stayed here, Carl. What's that all about?"

"I thought she'd be safe."

Pete's voice rose a notch as he said, "Any of this remind you of your behaviour when we worked together in Belleford?"

North reacted instantly. "Belleford was completely different."

Pete looked sceptical. "You're working alone. It's this white knight nonsense all over again, and a woman's this close to dying." Pete held his right thumb and forefinger half an inch apart.

North picked up Pete's cigarette package and fired it across the table. It bounced off Pete's chest. North stood and took a few steps toward the kitchen where two officers were dusting for fingerprints. He ran his fingers through his hair and returned to his chair. "Sorry. This has been a tough day."

Pete left the cigarette box where it had landed on the table after hitting his chest. "I assume drug tests will show marijuana in her system."

North nodded and didn't add anything.

"Did you smoke up with her?"

North shook his head.

"And you're willing to take a test to prove that?"

Tiredness came out of nowhere and washed over North. "Yes, of course."

"Why didn't you hold her overnight at the station? Or book her and have her sent to the London detention centre? You could have charged her with possession, maybe the intent to traffic. She'd have been in a secure environment for a while."

"That's obvious now, isn't it? But at the time, I did what we all do... the best I could under the circumstances."

"Your dick wasn't doing any of your thinking? When this hits the press, the public will know you had a stripper with you the night before an attempt was made on her life. How's that going to look?"

"You're saying I had sex with her and killed her to cover it up? I taped her to a chair and sent her over the balcony?"

A digital flash ignited in the living room, twice and then a third time. Pete turned to look in that direction, at Vandenberg and back at North. "Okay, let's get that one out of the way. Did you have sex with her and try to kill her to cover it up?"

"You're clearly delusional. I know a good psychiatrist that can help you with that." But inside himself, North remembered how close he had been to a different answer to the first part of the question.

"Did you take her to bed with you?"

"We did not have sex."

Pete raised his eyebrows but otherwise did not comment.

"We did not exchange bodily fluids," North said. "If there is evidence of sex or sexual assault, do all the DNA testing you want, you won't find any samples pointing to me."

"You're volunteering your DNA?"

"Of course."

Pete's eyes moved from Jennifer to Vandenberg. "So where does that leave us?"

Vandenberg said, "They found a quantity of marijuana in your front closet, Carl."

North said, "I told you, Candy was smoking up."

"Did she need a couple of kilos?"

North hoped his face didn't reveal how unnerved he felt by this news. "I don't know what you're talking about."

"Was that quantity of marijuana here last night?"

North brushed one palm over his short hair, several times. "She had an overnight case. It could have been in there."

"The drugs were on a shelf in your closet, in a zip-lock bag."

North said, "A couple of kilos would be pocket change to those bastards."

"We've got some serious challenges here." Vandenberg was addressing Pete and Jennifer.

North said, "Do we really..."

Vandenberg didn't let him finish his sentence. "All this has to be run by the chief. But the public is quite prepared to think the worst."

An Identification Officer approached Vandenberg. The staff sergeant left for the small kitchen and had a private conversation. Two officers exited the balcony and closed the sliding door. Jennifer rubbed her sleeves and said, "Maybe it'll start to warm up in here again."

Vandenberg returned to his chair. "As for your conduct last night... Ignoring for a moment the attempted murder of this Candy, there definitely is a question of unprofessional conduct. It's not helped by drugs in your apartment, including two smoked roaches."

North said, "There are extenuating circumstances."

"The decision to invite a possible witness to your apartment. That alone could skew an investigation and a trial. No matter who tried to kill her, a good defense lawyer will use anything and everything to throw doubt on the case for the Crown. Am I wrong about that?"

Nobody argued.

"Then there are our friends in the media. I'm surprised nobody's been here from the *T-J.*"

Pete said, "I hear the *Times-Journal* is so short-staffed, their own building could burn down, and they'd have nobody to cover it."

Jennifer asked, "What if somebody from this apartment building called them?"

Pete's eyes narrowed, and he glanced away. "We'll check that as we're canvassing apartments. This could look like a suicide attempt. The media tend to tiptoe around that subject."

"She was taped to a chair," Jennifer said. "How can that possibly look like suicide?"

"She fell from a balcony." Pete smiled bitterly at the table. "Who knows about the taped-to-a-chair part?"

"The medics and anybody who looked down from their balcony or happened to walk by."

"What about the London media?" Vandenberg asked. "The *Free Press*? TV or radio?"

Jennifer said, "Nobody's got a bureau in St. Thomas any more."

Vandenberg asked a different question. "How long have you lived in this apartment, Carl?"

"Moved in just before Christmas."

Two uniformed officers seemed to be wrapping up their initial search of the apartment. The Identification Officer would be here for at least two more hours. Vandenberg said, "People's heads are all over the place around Christmas. It may not be common knowledge that a St. Thomas police officer was living in this apartment."

North said, "Possible, but they don't call this Gossip Central for nothing."

"Point taken. We'll keep this as low-key as we can, talk about injury from a fall, foul play has not been ruled out, the investigation is ongoing. What's this, Wednesday? I get confused when there's a holiday."

"Wednesday, Sir," Jennifer grinned. "All day. Sorry, couldn't resist."

"It's the chief's call on how we handle the media. I'm going to recommend a release as late today as we can manage. The London media will pay little or no attention to a fall in St. Thomas. If it's late today, with the *T-J's* deadlines, it won't be picked up before Thursday. Run in the paper at the soonest Friday. With any luck, we have until Monday before any follow-up stories."

Jennifer said, "The *Free Press* might pick it up from the *T-J*, with the Sun Media common ownership thing."

Vandenberg changed the subject. "If there's a suspension, you'll face that next week, Carl."

"Appreciate the timing but not the thought." North reached for another cigarette. He lit it with Pete's lighter. His fingers were shaking. "Why would you suspend me?"

"It's patently ridiculous that you would tie a woman to the chair and so on. We know that. But if there is additional evidence against you, or if this thing starts to look damaging to the reputation of Police Services, we will have no choice."

If it had been any other officer, North would have agreed whole-heartedly. He knew they wouldn't find his prints on the plastic bag of marijuana. There were possibilities here. It looked as if he had two days plus the weekend.

"Should the woman die, everything changes again." Vandenberg stood and prepared to leave. "One last thing, Sergeant North. And I want strict adherence to this. You are not to be involved with the investigation into the woman who was injured here today. That also applies to the strip clubs and their owners. You come anywhere near those files, and it's the end of your career with us. Is that understood?"

"Perfectly," said North, and he was not lying. A world of difference lay between understanding something and agreeing to it.

"Why don't you take some personal time? Thursday and Friday, plus the weekend, until we see how things shake out?" said Vandenberg. "Paid time. I'll call your cell phone Sunday night and let you know about next week."

## CHAPTER 16

A police officer, and more particularly, a possible suspect, could not continue living in a crime scene. North suggested another apartment in Grand Central. Vandenberg said a few nights at the Comfort Inn—Talbot and Centennial at the east end of St. Thomas—were not going to finish off the police budget for the year.

Using an unmarked car, North transported clothes, toiletries, file folders, police paraphernalia and two novels to the hotel. He checked in, threw everything on the bed and returned to his unmarked Crown Vic. He drove through a winter evening, not snowing, temperature falling. He stopped at Simpson's Variety on Wellington for cigarettes and a lighter.

He smoked two duMauriers during the drive to Swiss Chalet on Talbot, the driver's window letting in the dreaded cold. The first cigarette seemed tasteless, but the second, ignited from the glowing end of the first, gave him a buzz. Another storm was in the offing. A winter chill seemed to penetrate his bones.

After a quarter-chicken dinner and two beers, North was drowsy. A hot coffee didn't perk him up. He was drifting off in the warmth of the restaurant. He woke from a brief dream involving pursuit down corridors of a town hall in his native Saskatchewan. He lifted his chin off his palms. Serving noises from the half-full restaurant clattered around him. Nobody seemed to have noticed his nap. He paid by debit, left, and headed the car west on Talbot Street for a take-out coffee from the drive-through. The caffeine, with his after-supper cigarette, lifted his heart rate. The Beer Store was two blocks further west. He bought a chilled twenty-four of Lakeport.

Back at the Comfort Inn, North took a long, hot shower. Streaming water beat against the cords running from his neck to his shoulders. When he finished, his calves were red and itching. He applied cool lotion. Naked except for a T-shirt, he unpacked some clothing into tan-coloured cupboard drawers and hung shirts and pants in a closet by the bathroom.

At 8:00 p.m., he opened a beer and a file folder. He read three paragraphs on the Campbell fire. The words made no sense. He started again. Paragraphs danced and faded in front of his eyes. Closing the file, he dialled the front desk on a beige telephone set, asked for a 7:00 a.m. wake-up call, turned off all the lights, got into bed and beat the pillow with his fist— why hadn't he brought his own? He found a black remote. The television glowed in the room, inviting him to sample movies, including XTV. That would look terrific on his expense claim. Changing channels, he found *CSI*, tried to watch it. His eyelids drooped.

A man was hammering and hammering on the side door of the police station. Candy, wearing a peacock costume, her small breasts exposed and thrusting at him, slid the door sideways. "Who you are?"

"Sergeant North."

Candy checked a list, smiled and walked ahead of him, hips rotating in a sparkling bikini bottom. He followed her through a confusing warren of staircases and hallways. Except for Constable Jennifer working at her desk in a police constable's hat—and nothing else—the squad room was empty. North had never seen anyone so beautiful, so physically perfect. He approached, leaned over. Jennifer smiled up at him, an index finger raised. Her accent was East European. "Look but not touch. Only police mens, they may touch."

"I am the police."

Jennifer pulled out a clipboard. "Not on sheet. Are you checking with front desk?"

North was aroused by this Jennifer/Candy woman. He loved her. "I paid at the front."

"Okey-dokey. Just once, for you. The price, she is very high."

North reached to caress a nipple with two fingers. His left hand moved to circle his gigantic erection. He and the woman rose to the top floor of a skyscraper. White light glowed behind Jennifer/Candy. Snow flowed past her hair. The floor beneath her dissolved. Her face was elongated. North reached for her. She was pulling him. There was no support, no floor, no protective railing. With her, North began to fall.

At 11:07, according to the large red dial on the bedside clock radio, the telephone beeped, and North woke with a start, semi-paralyzed. His heart raced. On the television set, a slim blond woman in a long black leather coat offered earnest comments about nuclear build-up in Iran. North forced himself to roll toward the telephone. His throat was dry. "Hello." He sat on the edge of the bed and felt disoriented.

"Is that you, sweets? Your voice sounds funny."

The bedspread and television and outline of curtains seemed to move around him. An indistinct ringing sounded in his left ear. He sucked on his false front tooth and forced himself to stand. "Give me a minute."

North set down the receiver. His heart was scary fast. In the bathroom, he ran cold water and drank two small glassfuls. The figure in the mirror depressed him. Why hadn't he made more progress on the fitness front? Cigarettes weren't going to help.

Returning to the desk between his bed and the window, he muted the television and picked up the receiver. "How'd you get this number?"

"I called the station and told them who I was. Where were you just now? I thought you were never coming back."

"I got some water."

"I'm all worried about you. Before, like yesterday, I called your apartment, there was no answer, so I left a message, and you never called back. Are you okay?"

He wasn't okay. He was barely hanging on. "Yeah, I'm fine. I had to vacate my apartment for a while."

"What happened?"

"Police business. My boss thought it would be best."

"I know you can't tell me, but were you like threatened?"

"Sorry, all this is confidential." They were slipping back into old, familiar patterns. Connie wanted to know. He could only tell her so much. She overwhelmed him with her enthusiasm and her caring. He retreated. North had to be careful. It would be all too easy to weaken, see whether she might take him back. All their problems—or more accurately, every problem he had caused—would still be there.

"Maddy called. She hasn't heard from you, like hardly at all."

Except for that brief, awful lunch visit at Christmas, North hadn't seen the kids from his first marriage since the disintegration of his second. "I saw them over the holidays."

"Sounds like Maddy doesn't get along too good with her step-dad."

"I'm glad my ex found somebody willing to fund her lifestyle. She's become quite the artist since she hooked up with this dude. Why did Maddy call you?"

"I dunno. We became sort of close, when..."

North was drifting further away from his children all the time, now that they lived in Burlington. "You talk to Dylan?"

"Maddy says he's into a Goth phase. He wears black all the time, and he has a piercing."

"I went a little ballistic when I saw him."

"Maddy said you called him an idiot."

North cared about them. It was important that he have some presence in their lives. He couldn't leave it all up to first wife, Audrey, whom he'd dubbed "Odd" in the phase when she'd left him to live in the projects and date the type of guy he commonly arrested after Saturday night bar fights. "He looked like one. An idiot getting ready for Hallowe'en. I've got to get up to see them more."

"Does Odd still fight you over access?"

"Funny you should mention that. Last time we talked, I heard all about the benefits of shared custody. Like that's going to happen."

"Guilt does no good. I know that from the weight thing."

"Guess what I got them for Christmas? Gift certificates and candy. I had no idea what they might actually want. The three of us went to Mickey D's Café. It was one of the most depressing days in recent memory." To compensate, he'd made stupid jokes about other patrons. Maddy seemed to appreciate some of these. Dylan had sat in his chair, pale and dark, before erupting in inappropriate laughter he had trouble controlling.

"I lost 10 pounds."

"Good for you." That was a stupid thing to say. So he tried, "You didn't need to do that." Might not be enough. "Last time I saw you, you looked great."

"I'm walking a lot."

"I should get into that."

"I know we both made some..." Her voice thickened and stopped. A quick intake of breath, then another. "I told myself I wouldn't do this, and I won't."

North waited and then said, "Do what?"

"I'm not going to beg. We both said things we didn't mean. And I was really angry... But I forgot how much you meant to me."

"It's too soon, Con. It's just past the holidays. I get lonesome, too. But we can't do this."

"You're right. I just wanted to get that off my chest, and now you know..."

North didn't say anything.

"Maybe I can call you again some time, like just to talk."

North rubbed the indentation where his nose had been broken at hockey. He didn't know what to think. "Maybe."

After he'd hung up, North's mind was whirling. Would he ever get back to sleep? The beer was cool rather than ice cold. He drank one fast and the next two slower. When the late-night talk show changed, he crawled back under the covers.

There were escalators and small children. He was trying to save them. One little girl had dark hair and a flowered dress. The escalators speeded up. People with bony foreheads were in pursuit. Baseball bats swung at them. Some had the devil in them. They went down. Others, less evil, were knocked to their knees, but not out. They bled. The escalators accelerated. He and the girl were in a room, high up. With a primitive club, he was striking bony-headed people on their foreheads. All but one of them dropped and slept. More advanced on him. Snakes wriggled at their feet, over their shoulders, into their ears.

As he emerged from the dream, his heart rhythm was back up. It felt as if devils were surrounding him, entering people. They weren't particularly smart, these people with devils in them. But they were relentless.

A knock on his door spooked him. According to the bedside clock radio, it was 4:10 a.m.

## CHAPTER 17

North peered through his fish-eye lens peephole, groaned and leaned his
back against the wall.

Knocking continued, insistently.

"Just a minute," North called out. And more quietly, to himself, "Just
a goddamn minute."

Further tapping on the door. Connie's voice was muffled. "Carl."

North pulled on blue jockey shorts below a white T-shirt. He opened
the door.

"I got you a double double. I switched to black."

Connie surveyed the room. She set the coffees on a bedside table,
peeled off a green suede coat and tossed it over a suitcase on the bed. She
was wearing a brown dress with black and gold stitching in vertical patterns. It emphasized her bosom, looked good on her. Connie sat on a chair
by the desk and swung her legs back and forth like a little girl. She had on
black pumps—must have changed from boots in her car. The shoes and the
dress, North couldn't recall from before.

His mouth tasted like the bottom of a dumpster that had been too
long in the sun. His short dark hair must be a bed-headed mess. He did-
n't say anything, didn't trust himself to do that.

North went to the bathroom and ran the cold tap. He tossed his toiletries into a black zippered bag and picked up towels from the floor, drap-
ing them over the tub and a wall hanger. He drank a full glass of water and
brushed his teeth. Running water into his cupped hands, he splashed some
over his head, settling down the hair. He returned to the main room and
sat on the side of the bed, about the middle, so he could reach the coffee.
If he shifted his body, his legs would touch hers.

"Thanks for the coffee."

"You're welcome."

"You had quite a drive."

Connie shrugged her shoulders. "Not that far."

"You could have called first."

"Would you have seen me?"

"Maybe, maybe not." North took a long drink of tepid coffee, and
then another. In three more gulps, he finished two thirds of it. He was wide
awake, his body charged with caffeine.

"We never really got a chance to finish."

Emotions crowded in on North. "That wasn't exactly my fault. We were trying to work things out. Next thing I know, my lawyer is talking to yours."

"Maybe I got some bad advice. Maybe I was listening to other people, when I should have been listening to myself."

"Yeah, well, I don't find knowing yourself as easy as it's cracked up to be." North took another long drink of coffee. He didn't like this conversation, didn't want to be in the same room with her. He said, "I need to grab a shower."

With hot water streaming over his naked body, North thought about old times with Connie. Showering, knowing she was waiting for him. His eager, big-breasted wife. In bed, they had been good together.

As he dried himself, he was half-aroused. He slipped into a terrycloth robe. Was it sufficiently bulky that he wouldn't embarrass himself? What was Connie really doing here?

As soon as he left the bathroom, he had one answer.

The television set was glowing. On the screen, a fit, naked man was receiving oral ministrations from two women with big hair, one blond and one brunette. They were taking turns. They appeared to be enjoying themselves.

Connie patted the covers. "Time for your New Year's present, swee'-pea."

Too late now.

The movie was going to look good when he turned in his hotel expenses.

What the hell? Might give some prude in accounting a thrill.

## CHAPTER 18

Connie was on her side. Her fingers played with the hairs around his navel. "You lost weight."

North's left hand cupped the back of her neck. His fingers gently massaged the softness. "Not eating as regular as I used to."

"I was worried that might happen."

"I started smoking again."

"Oh, sweets, sorry to hear that." A pause and she said, "I smelled it when I came in."

North moved away, sat up and swung his legs over the side. Dizzy, he stayed in that position while his head settled down. "If I was like those movie guys, we could do it again."

He heard movement on the bed. Fingers trailed lightly up and down his spine. "Plenty of time for that."

Without replying, North leaned forward, switched on a bedside lamp, found the silver package and his lighter and ignited a cigarette. He turned off the light and swung back onto the bed, the end of his smoke glowing.

"Isn't smoking in bed dangerous?"

"Not compared with what we've just been through."

Her hand had found his cheek and was stroking it. "We're still married. We can do whatever we want."

"Just the thought of..."

"What?"

North switched on the light and butted his smoke. He extinguished the light and moved close to Connie. "You had your New Year's present, but we missed Christmas."

He had her turned away from him, was coming up inside her, when he realized how angry he was.

★

North slept briefly and went to the bathroom. When he came out, Connie was snoring gently. He finished two beers quietly at the desk in the room and thought. He crawled carefully in beside her. He slept until 7:00 when he woke with a mild headache, feeling heavy from far too little sleep and far too many feelings, all of them mixed.

The hotel offered a continental breakfast at the top of a set of stairs leading to the lobby. North drank three coffees to chase the wool from his head and ate four slices of toast with peanut butter and jam.

North's mind turned to his dilemma at work. Maybe the key was not in the incident at his apartment. Maybe it lay in New Year's Eve, in the two fires that night. He called Constable Tom Skelding's home number, got his answering machine and didn't leave a message. He pulled the notebook from his shirt pocket, found a number and dialled the man's cell. A computerized female voice invited him to leave a message, so North did. He said he was sorry to hear about Tom's suspension, he had a question or two, and invited Tom to return his call.

North went to his room. Connie was in the shower. While he waited for her to finish, he watched two women who looked like they should be in soap operas pitch some body stocking that appeared to be a clever reinvention of a girdle.

He donned blue slacks, a dress shirt and a maroon tie. Towelling her hair, Connie emerged from the steaming bathroom. His bathrobe was belted around her. She had applied pink lipstick unevenly. Her plump face looked lined and tired. Her bare feet had been reddened by the heat. "Mornin', sweets." She offered him a kiss, which he returned with stiff lips.

He said, "Old habits die hard."

Connie misunderstood this and smiled at him.

North asked, "You working today?"

"The nail business is not exactly booming the week after New Year's. I took the day off. I could have the week if I need it."

What did that mean? North said, "I have to get going."

"What time you back, Carl?"

"Not sure."

"This doesn't have to mean anything."

"Okay."

"Even if it does to me."

"Jeez, Con."

"You sound pissed off." Connie's lips tightened.

So many possible sarcastic answers occurred to North, he decided the wise thing was to say, "Gotta go."

He strapped on his shoulder holster, grabbed his parka and his cigarettes, did not kiss her goodbye and ran downstairs to his unmarked car. He scraped an area of his frosted windshield about two feet across and one foot high, and had to duck his head in different positions to see enough to drive. He turned west on Talbot Street. Out of habit, he was heading toward the station. He had his first cigarette of the day going, the window two inches down to let smoke escape, when his cell rang. Tom Skelding's deep "Hello" lacked the man's usual warmth and enthusiasm.

North repeated what he'd said in his message, about how sorry he was.

Tom said, "I have no idea who to believe right now."

"I'm doing this on my own." North's defroster was warming his windshield from the bottom. "Nobody knows I'm making this call."

"I feel so much better, now that we've cleared that up."

"Sarcasm, sarcasm. The first sign of a very frustrated individual." The stoplight at First and Talbot turned red. North's car slid to a stop behind a white panel truck, its right blinker flashing. The truck's exhaust pipe emitted billowing clouds. "I've always had a lot of respect for you. With what you're going through, it wouldn't hurt to talk to somebody."

"What's this, your police psychology act?"

"With all the crap we face, we have to be psychologists. Problem is, some of us won't admit when *we* need help."

There was a lengthy pause before Tom said, "What's your point?"

"I've got a few problems of my own. They pulled me off the investigation of the New Year's deaths. I'm pretty much suspended." That was a slight exaggeration, but would Tom know the difference? "There's something rotten in Denmark."

"Like that's news to me."

"I want to talk to you, understand as much as I can, starting with the night of the fires. Maybe we can help each other."

A long silence on the phone before, "I'll be at the house all morning."

"I can be there in a few minutes." The truck ahead of North was turning right. He entered the intersection. Tom's place was in the upscale Lake Margaret subdivision. North said he'd be there inside 15 minutes.

North called the station. He asked reception to pass along regrets for the morning meeting. Why had he done that? He was on paid personal leave time.

At the lights by Eastside Mario's, he turned into a parking lot for big box stores, circled around and drove back east on Talbot. At Fairview, he turned south and drove until he could see snow-drifted farmland and the new Faith Baptist Church and school ahead on his left. His car slid right onto Axford Parkway.

After two more turns, he arrived at Tom's two-storey with double garage in front. Interest rates were low, but it was it curious a constable like Tom could afford a new home of this size in Lake Margaret. When they'd worked together, they'd become friendly, and Tom had revealed some of his personal situation. Married, two young kids. Unlike North, he didn't have ongoing legal bills and monthly child support payments. Still, a house worth almost $500,000, a late-model Cadillac Escalade and a black Jeep sitting in the driveway? North hadn't considered this before. Tom's wife, Rebecca, worked at St. Thomas Elgin General Hospital, but only part-time.

A perky woman, blond hair pulled back in a ponytail, answered the door. She extended a firm handshake, and her mouth opened in a smile that revealed even, white teeth. "Tom said you were coming over, Carl. Don't stand out there in the cold." The smile broadened; she tried a chuckle as if what she had said were funny, but she frowned immediately after. "C'mon inside. You want a coffee?"

"Not unless Tom does." His shoes dripped melting snow on a mat with a picture of a moose lifting its head in a swamp. A skylight in a cathedral ceiling above him let in brilliant winter sunshine.

Becky turned and called, "Tom. Carl's here." She looked good in a turquoise jogging suit. She might even run in one. She was doing something to keep the shape of a 20-year-old.

Tom Skelding's face was so pale it seemed more light green than white. Red blotches showed on his cheeks, as if he hadn't slept. He was unshaven. His brown eyes were glazed with pink. They shifted from North to morning light glowing through a glass semi-circle above the front door, to a closet off to one side, and back to North. "Beck's getting the kids ready for school. Let's do this in the Jeep."

"Sure," North said. "You should grab a jacket. It's a little nippy."

Tom took two awkward steps forward. He faced North, towering above him. He was less than a foot away. His breath was strong, unpleasant. "Take off your coat. Please. I have to do this, even to you."

North stared at the man's mottled face, uncomfortably close. He unbuttoned his parka and flung it over one arm. Tom ran his fingers over North's shoulder, his torso, down his back, then his legs, one at a time. He felt his tie, checked the inside of his belt. In one smooth motion, he removed North's weapon from his shoulder holster and said, "I'll get a coat. We'll talk in the vehicle."

Tom pulled a winter coat out of a closet with sliding doors and slipped North's gun into a side pocket. North said, "You going to give me back my piece? Or do I have to take it away from you?"

Tom's smile seemed forced; his teeth were yellowed. His smile stopped. "I wouldn't make threats I couldn't carry out. But that's me."

The Jeep was modelled after the original, designed for war. It was a T-J, favoured by young men who loved to roar into Port Stanley on a summer day to pick up women or impress other guys with six-pack abs and tans and colourful shorts bagging to their knees. A beach toy for a single man 10 years younger than Tom. This one was black. As it roared to life, the fan belt screamed. Tom let it idle for two minutes, until the screeching stopped. He was twitchy, shifting on the seat as he said, "We'll drive to Tims, and I'll buy you one. Guess one more won't kill me."

"So far, this seems to be your show, Tom."

The constable slammed the vehicle into reverse. The Jeep wound its way past homes twinkling with frost in the sunlight. Paths to the street had been shovelled or snow-blown. Suburbia was waking up, venting smoke from chimneys and tailpipes.

North said winter wasn't his favourite season. Tom waved this off, so North didn't attempt any more conversation until they were in the drive-through at First and Elm. "I call it the drive-trough," North said.

Tom grunted.

"You want to give me back my piece?" North asked.

"Let's get out of Dodge." Tom paid the cashier, and they left, turning east on Elm. The four-wheel-drive vehicle skidded as he passed a nervous senior with black-gloved hands gripping the wheel of a tan Buick Century.

North drummed his fingers on the door. "You know what you do to an officer when you take his weapon."

The Jeep turned right on Fairview and zoomed through the residential neighbourhood, passing vehicles. They were doing 100 kilometres an hour in a 60 zone before they reached the edge of the city with Faith Baptist Church on their left and the entrance to St. Joseph's High School and Fanshawe College on their right. Skeletal lights spiked above snow-crusted ball diamonds. Tom was at 120, then 130 on the two-lane highway, as they left the city limits.

"Where's the fire?" North said. "You want to slow it down a little?"

"Doesn't make any difference."

North tried putting authority in his voice. "Give me back my piece."

Tom took his eyes off the road and rummaged the weapon out of his coat pocket. He pointed it at North before replacing it.

North contemplated making a play for it and decided against it. Tom had North on both size and strength. And at the speed they were travelling, a wrestling match could be disastrous. "You want to kill us both?"

No reply.

"A little drug trouble isn't the end of the world."

Tom raised his eyebrows and pasted on a sarcastic smile. "Glad you shared that. I feel so much better."

Tom braked abruptly, the vehicle skidding. He pumped the brakes again and fishtailed right onto Fruit Ridge Line, brushing a snowbank. He immediately hit the gas pedal. The Jeep accelerated to 110. A farmer was snow-blowing a long lane running south off the road, the white effluent arcing in a steady curve. There was no other traffic.

North asked, "Where we going?"

"West."

"I can see that. You want to tell me where?"

"Finish your coffee. You may need it."

North took a sip. "I need to take a whiz. Can we stop?"

Tom increased his speed to 125. Frost was creeping in an elaborate curlicue pattern up North's side window. "I called you because I was sorry to hear about your suspension."

"You must be the only one. Nobody else gave a rat's ass."

"You want to talk about it?"

"It's like being dead. What's there to say?"

"I don't know."

"No, you don't. Nobody does."

"Try me."

"What if you married a woman who was used to a certain style?"

"We're talking about Becky?"

"Let's say her father owned his own business. You should see the home she grew up in."

"Every high school kid knows police officers have access to drugs."

"Doesn't mean I took anything."

"We're like bank tellers with cash. There's so much of it, why not nip a little on the side? Am I close?"

Tom didn't respond. His shoulder slumped to the left against the door. He was steering with his right index finger when they roared across Sunset Road, ignoring the stop sign. They missed a snow plough by about four seconds.

North wanted to scream at him.

A weak smile played around Tom's mouth. He wiped at his lips as if he had detected drool. He sipped from his brown coffee cup.

"What about your kids?"

Tom took something out of his pocket and swallowed it with coffee.

"This is crazy." North slammed a fist against the passenger door, hurting his knuckles.

They careened down roads, most of which North didn't recognize. When he first met Tom, the man had been self-assured, even charming to both women and men. He never seemed to resort to force or bullying. His smile and his good looks seemed to do his work for him. No comparison with the man who was now driving the Jeep.

A green sign pointed toward Shedden. From the position of the sun, they seemed to be heading northwest.

Somewhere in this vast rolling farm landscape so white it could be blinding, they topped a hill and burst upon a school bus with a yellow arm extended, flashers going. Tom steered left, roaring past it, oblivious.

North yelled at him, "Slow down."

Tom was back to steering with one finger. "Speed, it's the only thing. You just do it and do it and do it."

They flew up an overpass above the 401. Some time later, Tom slowed for a left turn. North lunged for the steering wheel. With the strength that charges through people who are beyond fear, Tom shifted his body on the seat, blocked North and shoved him away.

Half a mile down a snow-covered gravel road, Tom pulled into a grove. Spruce trees were laden with snow. A bright red cardinal lifted from a branch. Tom killed the engine. North had trouble believing the quiet. His ears rang in the stillness. He said, "I wish you would talk to me."

Tom pulled North's weapon out of his pocket. An uneasy smile failed to fully establish itself on his lips. He ejected a bullet, put it back in. He raised the weapon to North's left temple.

North couldn't help himself. He shrank away. When he tried to speak, something lodged in his throat. He coughed and said in what he hoped was a calm voice, "You want to give me one for no good reason?"

Tom hissed, "Shut up."

"Okay, okay, you do the talking."

Tom whipped his head side-to-side, close to tears. "You have no idea. Nobody does." The features of his face scrunched up. "Everybody runs and hides. Everybody. Even you. Even the police association."

"I called you, Tom."

Tom bounced the mouth of the weapon against North's temple for emphasis. North's head ached from the contact. Tom said, "You could be a plant. How do I know? How do I have any fucking idea?"

"Say you're right." North's heart was a tiny, active drum working an erratic rhythm in his chest. "Say I was a plant, which I'm not, but just as a hypothetical, let's say I was. Is that why you're thinking about offing me?"

Tom shoved the weapon once, hard, against North's head before he dropped it, into the crotch of his own pants. North was breathing hard. He managed to say, "You have anything in mind here?"

"You'll see. You'll all see." The gun stayed in Tom's lap as he turned the key. The Jeep started right away. He revved the accelerator. "A gun to your head? That's nothing. You should see what some of us go through every day."

"Okay, Tom." North breathed out through his nose. "Let's slow things down a little."

"Get out of the vehicle."

"I have no idea where I am, and you want to drop me off?"

"Trust me, you don't want to hang around for this next part."

"What next part?"

Tom's hands trembled. "There is a point to all this. You promise me, you'll remember? You won't forget what I said. There was a point to all this."

"I won't forget."

"Good. Now get out."

"I can't do that."

"Oh, Jesus. Jesus, Jesus. Don't make me." He raised the weapon. The barrel was moving in North's direction.

North swallowed and said, "I'm leaving, Tom. See, I'm opening the door." North was outside. He stepped into a drift half way to his knee. "Shit," he grunted. Snow rode above his ankles, melted inside his pant legs.

He closed the door. Using the side of the Jeep for balance, he took long strides to the back. He glanced back from time to time, watching for movement, the glint of a weapon. He followed the vehicle's tracks to the gravel road, turned left and started walking. The centre was packed, slippery in parts. North wished he were wearing Kodiaks.

The Jeep backed out of the lane, leaving the shelter of the conifers. It turned away from North and disappeared over a knoll. North kept walking. His cheeks tingled, his nose ran, and his lips felt numb. He stamped his feet to maintain circulation. His ears ached, and he rubbed them.

Birds called to each other, sounding cheerful. A small, black flock landed in some cedars. He heard scratching from that grove—some animal he had no desire to meet. He set off and trudged past farms with newer brick houses or the older, century style, all well-maintained. Barns had been painted and repaired, late-model vehicles in driveways. According to signs at the road or on mailboxes, most of them were owned by McCallums.

After 20 minutes, he came to an intersection that had green road signs with white lettering. He was at the junction of Iona Road and Aberdeen Line. Corn stalks sprouted in broken, curving rows from a field with vast, undulating drifts. In a farmyard near the corner, a pen of light and dark calves exhaled white streams of steam. A crow with black feathers with a purple sheen landed in a tree and scolded North. He yelled back. The bird listened about as well as Tom.

### CHAPTER 19

With stiff, shaking thumbs, North punched in the number for the St. Thomas police station on his cell. He asked Jennifer Duchamps to pick him up before frostbite killed him. He told her where he was.

"Are you hung over? Or still drunk?"

"Neither. But 20 below seems to give you a new headache."

"I'm driving half way across Elgin County just because you ask me to?"

"In a word, yes."

She hesitated before saying, her tone muffled, "You're near the Pythons. That's OPP territory."

"Like I'm going to call the OPP." He switched to a child's voice. "I'm turning into a Popsicle in your jurisdiction. Please, please pick me up."

Jennifer laughed and lowered her tone to the point that North could barely hear her. "This has nothing to do with the health and safety problem on your balcony, right?"

"I'm shocked you would suggest such a thing."

"I'll be there as soon as I can."

"Icicles are forming on icicles under my nose. Grab a car, and get your ass out here."

"I love how you sweet-talk me into things."

Jennifer arrived within 30 minutes, with a warm coffee in a brown container. Inside the vehicle, shaking, wrapping his fingers around the coffee, North said, "You're an angel. If Marcel ever lets you go, I'm first in line."

"What makes you think I'd want you?"

North's trembling wouldn't let up. "Natural good looks. Sense of humour. Animal magnetism."

She pulled three tissues from a box on the seat. "Nothing sexier than a nose running like a fountain."

She asked, "Are we idling the vehicle to add holes to the ozone? Or are you going to tell me what's going on?"

"Let's give it a minute. I'm actually beginning to feel my toes."

"What's next, the brain? That'd be a shocker."

"Intelligence being your strong suit, you want to tell me why Tom would drive me all the way out here and drop me off?"

"Tom Skelding?"

"Yes."

"He dropped you off here? How did that happen?"

He went over his call to Tom, the visit to his house, the officer's condition, the wild winter ride.

"Did you get your piece back?"

"No." North finished his coffee and crushed the cup. His gloves were on the seat beside him. He rubbed his hands together over hot air flowing from a vent.

"He went in that direction." North pointed west.

Jennifer put the car in gear. She drove past the McCallums', and past the lane to the bush where Tom had dropped North. Less than a kilometre down the road, a Jeep showed black against a landscape undulating white and blue and silver to the horizon.

The vehicle was parked on the road near the end of a laneway. A heavy wrought-iron metal gate, hinged to a stone pillar, shut off access to that laneway, which led to a set of farm buildings on their right. The largest building in the yard was an old barn. Its siding was weathered, with the occasional board missing. A huge, round symbol—intertwining snakes—had been painted on a wide wooden door.

Three snowmobiles were parked inside a vinyl-covered shed, dome-shaped. The house was two-storey, frame, needing paint. Its roof was steep and had been redone with bright green metal.

An American Confederate flag drooped, red and black on white, from a tall pole to the east of the house. Two enormous Rottweilers woofed as the cruiser came close to the gate. "That's right," North said. "Stay up by the barn. Why did you take a marked vehicle?"

"It was all they had." Jennifer's tires squeaked on snow as they approached the Jeep.

"That's him," North said. "Or it sure looks like his Jeep." A figure was slumped behind the steering wheel. No movement was visible through the four-wheel-drive's tinted windows. Exhaust streamed from its tailpipe.

Jennifer stopped, and North used a level, police-procedural voice. "Remain with the vehicle."

"Is that an order?"

North glanced at her and said in the same borderline monotone, "Suit yourself."

The two of them exited and slammed car doors almost in unison. Jennifer patted herself, checking to make sure she had everything she should be carrying. This door-closing attracted attention in the farmyard. Resuming their deep-throated barking, the dogs loped down the lane toward Jennifer and North.

At the house, a slim man in jeans and a white sleeveless T-shirt leaned out a side door and whistled, twice, shrilly. The dogs slowed. The man whistled once more. They turned, yapped to show their dissatisfaction with this command, and padded toward the house, tongues lolling.

North was at the Jeep before Jennifer. Blood spattered the side window. He opened the driver's door. His teeth clenched, his insides turned over, there was a tremor in his fingers. "Jesus, don't look."

The ignition key alarm beeped steadily. Jennifer approached the far side of the vehicle.

North's words spilled out. "Nothing to be gained by seeing this."

Jennifer opened the passenger door, glanced once deliberately inside and turned away, her face becoming pale olive, her lips a tight line. One gloved hand went to her mouth. She twisted and bent over the snowbank, her diaphragm heaving. She straightened, wiped her mouth with the back of her glove. Her gaze shifted up to the horizon. Her cheeks were still pale but had lost their light green. Jennifer took several deep breaths, said, "Sorry, give me a minute."

The ignition key alarm beeped and beeped.

Jennifer walked slowly to her vehicle and sipped from her cold coffee cup.

Snow crunched. She came up behind North. She was against his back, one hand on his left shoulder. Through the bulk of his winter clothing, he was aware of her body.

"I'm just..." Her chest convulsed. Tears came.

North didn't move, and then he did. He swivelled and hugged her, crushing her face against his shoulder.

A man shouted from the house. "What the fuck's going on?"

North ripped himself away from her. He leaned in through the vehicle's door. He tried not to contact any part of Tom Skelding's body as he felt for the ignition, switched off the engine and pocketed the keys. The beeping ended. Jennifer brought her crying under control. Other than the steady hum of her cruiser, the raucous call of a crow from a tree, the slamming of a door at the house, it was quiet

"Is that your weapon?" Jennifer asked quietly, sniffing as she nodded her head toward the front seat of the Jeep.

A Smith and Wesson was in Tom's slack right hand. His thumb curved around the trigger.

The blood pattern people would go nuts over this one. A song lyric came to him. *Brains were on the sidewalk. Blood was on his shoes.* He focused on the weapon and said, "Far as I know, he didn't bring his. You okay to call this in, from your vehicle?"

"You thinking a 10-46?"

"Either that or 10-44. Probably 46."

*Brains were on the ceiling. Blood was on his hands.*

Jennifer's boots tramped the snow-crust at the side of the road. The crow cawed and flapped wide wings. A piece of paper was crumpled in Tom's other hand. North pried it loose. It was blood-sticky. North's gloves came away blotched, stained. He opened the paper. In pencil, in what looked like an elementary schoolboy's hand, Tom had scrawled,

> *Carl,*
> *Tried to get Turk*
> *Screwed up again*
> *Becky deserves better*
> *Tell her for me, okay*
>           *Tom*

Tom never had been much for paperwork.

*Brains were on the, blood was on his.* Was it an Eaglesmith tune?

North eased himself away from the vehicle. The paper stuck to his right glove. He slumped by the side of the Jeep. Sadness and frustration crushed his chest and sought escape up his throat and into his nose, his eyes.

Jennifer's boots were marching. Crunch, crunch, crunch. North stood and steadied himself.

North blinked and gave her the note. He inhaled and exhaled, coughed, blew his nose, wiped his eyes, used more tissues around his nostrils.

He glanced at Jennifer through clearer eyes. He attempted a crooked smile and said in a thick voice, "Pull yourself together."

*Brains were on his, blood was on his.*

The songwriter came to him.

Not Fred J. Eaglesmith.

John Prine.

★

"Give me your piece."

"Where are you going?"

North didn't answer.

"If you're doing what I think you're doing..."

"Give me your piece. That's an order."

Jennifer complied. North went to the gates and rattled them. They were cast iron painted black, with wide hinges on each side. A chain with heavy links and a padlock secured them in the centre. "What the hell?"

North plunged through a drift, to the right of the gate. He seized a post and clambered over, careful not to catch his coat or pants on the barbed wire strung across the top. He landed in deep snow. His lower calves were instantly cold where his pants had been shoved above the tops of his boots.

"Hey, Carl."

Paying her no heed, he took galumphing strides through drifts until he reached the packed driveway. He stamped his feet. Behind him, Jennifer swore. He started toward the house. Creaking fence noises. A thump as she landed on his side of the fence. Plunging and then running feet. Heavy panting. The fog of her breath as she drew up beside him. "You could have waited."

North picked up the pace.

He approached the Confederate flag pole. The house was on his left, the barn to his right. Snowmobiles were parked near the door of a Quonset between the two buildings. North scanned each one in turn, searching for a shattered headlight. Inside the house, dogs bumped and scratched against a wooden exterior door, barking deeply and steadily. They were not released.

North followed a track to the right, toward the barn. Through missing barn boards, he spied a white cube van, parked on the second floor of the old barn. On the main floor, there seemed to be recent construction.

A screen door at the house swung open and banged against the side of the house. "What d'you two want?"

Rottweilers crowded past the man. Panting and barking, they loped toward the police officers. Jennifer grabbed North's sleeve and moved behind him.

North raised Jennifer's Smith and Wesson. He was both angry and calm. Easy to drop both dogs, one or two bullets apiece. *Time to get a gun.* An Eaglesmith tune, for sure. If Turk said one wrong word, he'd be next.

North raised his piece.

About 20 feet from North and Jennifer, the dogs skidded in the snow. They looked around, at the house, stared back at the officers with bright eyes, whimpered, dropped their heads and trotted toward Turk. He lowered a dog whistle. "You two are trespassing."

"You know anything about a deceased officer in a vehicle outside your gate?"

"I know squat. One thing we both know—if you don't have a warrant, you're in deep shit. So produce or get lost."

"What's going on in that barn of yours?"

"A couple of machines being refurbished. All legal."

North considered his options. He raised his piece and sighted on Turk's forehead. One twitch of his index finger, that's all it would take. "Hey," Turk called to him. "You crazy?"

"Some people think so." North lowered the weapon.

A note of self-satisfaction in his voice, Turk yelled at their departing backs. "This is a free country. You can't go bargin' in on innocent citizens."

### CHAPTER 20

Within half an hour, one OPP cruiser, two cars from the St. Thomas police and an ambulance had arrived. Officers from St. Thomas included North's staff sergeant and a Forensics Identification officer, Greg Sernahan. Before the site became too trampled, North directed Constable Sernahan to a distinctive boot print, in packed snow between the Jeep and the ditch, plus others like it leading from the laneway. "I want some pictures, and do your best at a casting before the weather changes or some idiot walks through it."

"Yes, Sir. Lucky it's still here." The officer pointed at nearby tracks left by Jennifer and North.

"Sometimes we need a little luck. It looks like the print we got in the snow the night of the Campbell fire."

"We'll do what we can."

Officers yellow-taped an area around the Jeep, took measurements, searched for evidence and engaged in low-level murmured conversation. It was meticulous work and, at this crime scene, very contained. If it were a civilian death, after the first half hour so, North would have expected gallows humour from the officers. No laughter this morning. With grim steadiness, barely trusting themselves to glance at each other, the officers went about their work.

North was escorted to an OPP cruiser. He sat in the rear seat beside St. Thomas Staff Sergeant Norval Vandenberg. In front, OPP Constable Michelle Wong was behind the steering wheel. The motor was running, the heater on. Sunlight streaming through side windows added a pleasant thermal effect. Constable Jennifer Duchamps was being questioned in another cruiser.

Wong half-turned in her seat. Her skin was reddish brown as if she'd been tanning indoors or had returned from a Mexican vacation. Vandenberg opened with the usual: this was routine; nobody was under any suspicion. As soon as that was out of the way, North said, "Let's get one thing straight right up front. As far as I know, my weapon killed Constable Skelding."

Wong's brown eyes studied him in a not-unfriendly fashion. "Are you saying it is possible you killed Constable Tom Skelding?"

"Absolutely and categorically not. I was with Constable Duchamps when Constable Tom Skelding met his untimely end. From the note he left and what I observed prior to his death, it's almost certain he committed suicide."

Wong said, "The evidence points to that."

Vandenberg said, "Tell us about this ride you took with him."

North started with the telephone call to Tom after breakfast. He was careful to frame it in the context of personal follow-up with an officer he respected.

Vandenberg prickled at this explanation. "You placed a telephone call to a police officer when you knew he was under suspension for alleged drug violations? And you followed up on files when you were on personal leave time, with very specific parameters, i.e., stay completely away?"

"I admit it went a little beyond the personal. Tom was at the hotel fire in town. He has more background than anybody on what happened that night."

"You went to Constable Skelding's house." Wong continued writing as Vandenberg obviously struggled to keep his temper under control. "Were his wife and children present?"

"Yes, Sir."

"How did he seem?" Vandenberg's tone was curt.

"All nerves. Looked like he hadn't slept in days. He patted me down before we left."

"Was he after your weapon?"

"Not at first. When he knew I wasn't wearing a wire, he took my piece."

North reviewed the ride with Tom and his various attempts to reclaim his weapon. When he mentioned he'd seen Tom gulp something down with coffee, Vandenberg interrupted him, "Could you tell what it was?"

"No, Sir."

"That confirms the importance of the toxicology report." Vandenberg's emotions seemed to be under control. "When they do the autopsy, I mean."

Wong nodded. She had removed her hat. Her hair had a blue-black sheen.

Barking erupted near the farmhouse. A middle-aged woman in black leather fired up a snowmobile, rode down the laneway and opened the gate. A St. Thomas police vehicle drifted into the yard. Turk came to the door of the house. He whistled and shouted at the dogs, who galloped over to him. He was wearing a T-shirt that failed to cover a white strip of belly spreading above his jeans. One St. Thomas and one OPP constable left the white and blue cruiser and approached the house. Turk gesticulated emphatically, waving officers away.

North brought his attention back to the OPP cruiser. "Tom said we did not understand what he was going through." He pointed his right index finger at his temple, thumb raised. "He had my piece right here. That got my attention. He accused us of running and hiding, all of us. He thought we abandoned him."

The two officers left the farmhouse and headed back to the vehicle. The dogs settled down on snow drifts near the Quonset. "He said the police association wasn't there for him." North was trying to recall as much as he could of the conversation. "I tried to let him know that some of us still cared. That's why I called him."

Vandenberg was calm, his voice authoritative. "He sounds borderline paranoid."

"He was high. So mixed up, he didn't know his ass from his elbow. That's obvious from his note."

"Sounds like he had delusions of taking Turk down."

"Yeah." North hesitated. "It was weird the way he insisted there was a point to all this."

"Any idea what he meant?"

"At his worst, he didn't know who he was going to kill—me, Turk, or himself. But I think, in his own crazy way, he was trying to give us a link to the bikers."

Wong said, "You mean by driving to Turk's place?"

"Right. The woman who almost died at my apartment said somebody inside the force was spilling the beans. Turk hinted at the same thing. I hope like hell it wasn't Tom."

CHAPTER 21

Late Friday morning, less than one working day, plus the weekend, before North might face full suspension. He had left a message for Jennifer, and she hadn't called him back. North felt initial stirrings of unease, old feelings that could tilt into panic. He dressed quickly in outdoor gear and descended to the lobby area of the hotel. Outside was a claustrophobic world of swirling snow.

This blizzard deepened his unease. He stepped into the parking lot, turning east. His face was stung by raw wind; flakes and pellets whipped at him. Confronting the blast, he forced one foot in front of the other.

After Tom's decision to eat his weapon, St. Thomas officers had joined the OPP in executing a search warrant on Turk's place and the Amber Lee.

None of this was good for North, personally. Police officers believe that where there's smoke, a conflagration is lurking nearby. In North's case, the heat was increasing—beginning with Candy's brush with death at his apartment, followed by the discovery of a quantity of marijuana and two roaches. And now North's gun had killed Constable Skelding.

Running lights appeared and disappeared on the highway. A rectangular block emerged from the white squall. A transport truck braked for the lights at Centennial, red lights glowing. Maybe he should go further back, talk to Abe Friesen's wife again. But she would be such an unreliable witness. What about Abe himself? More hope there, if North had some leverage, could guarantee the Pythons would leave Abe and his family alone. To do that, the police needed solid evidence to implicate the bikers. And it might come, now that they had more reason to put pressure on Turk and the boys.

The wind was at North's back, snow driving past his ear protectors. He removed his right glove, rubbed his cheeks for warmth and replaced the glove.

Had Tom tried to implicate North, by using his weapon? Or was it simply convenient that North had shown up when Tom could see no way out?

Such thoughts were bleak and going nowhere. North concentrated on movement. One step, another step, another. At the west end of the lot, new drifts were sweeping across vehicle-high banks. He swung east again, his cheeks bitten by the wind. One step at a time. A few vehicles crept down the highway. None stirred in the hotel parking area.

He should call the hospital or stop around, see if he could talk to Candy. Maybe the search of Turk's place and the strip club this morning would solve everything. They'd find evidence linking the bikers to Tom's death and the other crimes since New Year's Eve. Why wasn't Jennifer returning his calls? Had she given up on him? Maybe she'd decided to keep her distance and save her career. North felt hemmed in, panicky.

North stomped his feet as he entered the lobby. Warmth hit him instantly. He unzipped his parka so he wouldn't immediately perspire.

A plump woman behind the reception desk was wearing a dark pantsuit and a white shirt with a wide collar. Her smiled reminded him of Connie's, the amused crinkling around the edges of her eyes. "A little wintry."

"Just a tad."

"There's coffee in the continental breakfast area."

North carried his coffee to his room. Connie's note, from the day before, was face-up on the desk:

*Dear Carl,*
*Glad we could get together.*
*I'll call you some time.*
                *Con*


No endearments, no "Love, Con."

The red light on the hotel room phone blinked. He stripped off his outside clothing, blew his nose and sipped his coffee before picking up the receiver to retrieve one message. Constable Duchamps wanted him to return her call at the station. She had an update on the searches.

He was patched through. After complaining about the weather, he asked if she was clear to talk. She was, although she sounded discouraged.

"Did anything turn up?" he asked.

"Almost nothing. The OPP seized a pair of boots in Turk's house. The tread resembles the print at the Campbell fire, maybe the one on your balcony. Almost certainly the impression we got from prints leading from Turk's laneway to Tom's Jeep."

"That's more than nothing."

Jennifer said, "It's circumstantial. How do we establish those are his boots and not somebody else's? How do we prove he was wearing them? The boot prints by Tom's Jeep are the weakest of all. So he went to the Jeep and had a look?"

"If he didn't call it in, that's something to work on Turk. Even if he didn't kill Tom."

"Not an easy man to work. We got phone records from his house and the strip club, but there are churches in this town that wouldn't come up as clean."

"The snakes knew we were coming?"

"Big surprise. Either there was nothing to start with, or they worked all night to remove it."

North took a sip of coffee and enjoyed the warmth all the way down. "It wasn't necessarily a leak from the department. After yesterday, it wouldn't take Einstein to figure out we were probably on our way."

"You know what really sucks? Skelding couldn't get anything right. The poor guy commits suicide outside their gate and leaves us this message pointing to the Pythons. But it's so blatant, it puts Turk on the alert."

North considered that. He picked up a ballpoint and started drawing circles and arrows on a hotel pad. "The man had problems. I wish I'd seen that sooner. Realistically, what did we expect to find at the farm? A drug distribution centre in the barn?"

"We had our hopes up. We were also hoping for a weapon—either there or at the Amber Lee—to match the AK-47 bullet found at the autopsy in Campbell."

"But you came up blank?"

"We found rifles, shotguns and handguns, all registered. Plus a small quantity of marijuana at the Amber Lee."

"How small?"

"Enough for a couple of joints."

"Perfect," North said. One of the designs he was inscribing on the pad had developed a face and horns. "Not enough for a trafficking charge. And no way to prove whose weed it is. You're sure there was no sign of a grow-op at the home of the Confederate flag?"

"You gotta love that flag. Listen, it's all verbal from the OPP at this stage, but apparently they came up dry."

"What about the distribution angle? Any signs of cocaine distribution or a crystal meth operation?"

"Let me see." There was a pause. Papers rustled over the telephone line. "There's propane heat to the barn, and there's a shell of a building constructed inside the main barn. Could be used for manufacture or distribution, but when the OPP arrived, it was set up like service bays. They found Harleys, snowmobiles and a white cube van. Nothing illegal."

North exhaled in frustration and reached for a cigarette. "So what's next?"

"We're meeting at 1:00 this afternoon to go over everything. Sometimes that helps. The mood around here's pretty bleak. First, Tom, and then this raid turns up next to zero."

"Funny, nobody sent me an invitation to your one o'clock meeting."

Jennifer chuckled, "It's in the mail. You're to RSVP."

"That meeting should end around 2:00." North lit the cigarette, rubbed his forehead and sucked on his false tooth. "I'll call you after that. Does anybody know you're talking to me? Just because I'm going down the toilet doesn't mean I have to take you with me."

Jennifer's voice faded, sounding distant as she called out, "Anybody know I'm talking to Gumper?" before her voice came back strongly, "There's only Pete here, and he says you got what you deserved."

"Tell him I love him, too. Who's following up on Tom Skelding?"

"OPP. Somebody's supposed to be here tomorrow."

"Where will they fit an investigator into the rat's maze?"

"It's a little crowded. We're getting a warrant for Tom's home, and we've impounded the Jeep."

North paused before he said, "The funeral's going to be tough. For the family and us."

"Police Services needs to have a presence. Some of us will go on a personal basis."

"Maybe I'll attend the visitation." Surely that didn't count as working on a file or following up in any way. "I was the last guy to see him alive. Unless Turk paid him a visit, of course."

"Wouldn't we love to establish that? So what are you doing? Catching up on daytime TV down at the love shack?"

"Why don't you join me?" North surveyed his room. With all his stuff, it was more crowded than the station. "I've got a queen-sized bed, and I'm getting lonesome. God, I'm starting to talk like Pierre. It's so bad, I actually went for a walk in this blizzard."

"The radio said it was supposed to end by noon. Seriously, are you working on any angles?"

"I don't have much. But I'd better think of something."

## CHAPTER 22

North called St. Thomas Elgin General Hospital. After following a voicemail trail, he reached a receptionist who told him Ivana Genska was a patient in ICU.

"Any visitors allowed?"

North was put through to the ward. When he explained to a nurse who he was, she told him there had been some progress overnight. Surgery had gone well, but the patient was in no condition to talk to anybody.

"What about the weekend? Any hope there?"

"My best advice is, check with us daily."

North slid back the heavy hotel curtains covering a wide window. Conical white shapes were building up from the bottom sill. Snow was drifting across the parking lot. The sky was more blue than white. Sunshine lit up a nearby farmer's field.

He dressed for the cold and took hotel stationery and a pen with him. He cleaned off the unmarked Crown Vic and drove to Wendy's—owned by the local Member of Parliament; it never hurt to schmooze in high places—for a spicy chicken filet combo. Over lunch, when he wasn't observing a seesaw battle between a truck trying to clear the lot and drive-through traffic, he jotted down everything that had happened since the New Year's Eve fires.

He organized names in a flow chart, a facsimile of the one his fellow officers would be using at their meeting, except they'd have photographs and computer print-outs and much more detail.

All paths led to the Pythons and to Turk. But where was the evidence? Where were the witnesses with the moxie to testify?

An enormous man with a ruddy complexion and a scarred left cheek bumped against three teenagers in the line-up and said, "Where ya think you're goin'?" Carrying a take-out coffee, he exited by the door near North. He was wearing a tattered snowmobile suit. As he left, he gave the sergeant a searing look.

North's gaze followed the man as he walked around the brick building. He wondered idly why the unfriendly giant hadn't left by the door on the far side, where he'd come in.

Returning to his papers, North reviewed the names on his rudimentary flow chart. He tried to be objective, analytical.

Was this a chain, and if so, was there a weak link?

Of the three women he'd interviewed, could any give sufficient evidence to put some bikers away?

Rachel Friesen said Abe's strip bar had been torched. Her husband had told her the bikers were determined to shut down his freelance activity. Possible supporting evidence. But North could envision no change there—Rachel hadn't agreed to testify, and even if she changed her mind, she might come across as borderline insane.

He tapped another name with his pen. Candy. There was a woman with plenty of motivation. If she were well enough to see this weekend, she might give him something.

Sarah McKinley.

No nuance in her world. No greys. She might be the key. Somebody with such a strong moral sense might be able to stand the pressure. And she had potential access. She was Duncan McKinley's mother.

A pale, pimple-faced young man with red hair, blue J-cloth in hand, approached North's small table and offered to take his tray. North surveyed him in a distracted way, gave him the remains of his lunch, and returned to his list of names.

How far would mamma bear go to protect her youngest cub?

Sarah's oldest son Jock had gone to Vancouver and never come home.

Her second son, Reggie, had committed suicide.

She had conceived Duncan when she was in her early 40s.

Iain, her husband, was dead.

About all Sarah had left, besides the farm and her indomitable will, was her youngest boy, Duncan. Could she be persuaded to help bring him in?

North pondered the woman's character as he stuffed paper and pen into his shirt pocket. He detected a faint odour off his parka. Past time to go to the cleaners.

The sun was a pale, hazy yellow in the northwestern sky, offering very little warmth. Three cars were in the west parking lot. Letters had been scratched into the frost on the rear window of his unmarked car: "FUCK U."

North muttered "Nice" before unlocking the vehicle, finding his long-handled scraper and vigorously removing the profanity from his window. The offending party could be anybody. But North's money was on the unfriendly giant.

North drove back to the hotel. His tires performed a minor dipsy-doodle at one slippery intersection. From his room, he dialled the station and was put through to Constable Jennifer Duchamps. "How'd the meeting go?"

Jennifer chuckled. "Deadly boring."

"So nothing new."

"You know the routine. Anything new on your end?"

"I've been thinking about Sarah McKinley."

"Your best buddy."

North emitted a short, sarcastic laugh and said, "We should talk to her again."

"Great minds think alike. Your boss and my close personal friend, Norval Vandenberg, assigned me and Pete to that call."

North considered this briefly as he was lighting a cigarette. "Are you going today? I'd like to be there with you."

"Nobody told me you couldn't come. You're smoking again, aren't you? It wasn't just that one night."

"Yeah, sort of."

"That's like claiming you're sort of pregnant."

"Wouldn't know. Never been pregnant."

Jennifer laughed, and North thought of spring, which would eventually arrive. Spring and flowers.

"Shut up," she said.

"That's no way to talk to the man who is technically your boss and has maybe a five percent chance of remaining so after Monday. Any reports back yet?"

"The fire at the strip bar, everything supports the arson theory."

"Rachel Friesen told us her husband's bar was torched. They could both be arson."

"I'm calling Sarah when I get off the phone. Even if she doesn't answer, we're going to head out there. I don't think she travels far from the ranch. We should be there by 4:30. Anything we should know in advance about how you want to approach this?"

"You know me. I don't like to script these things too closely." Partly to annoy Jennifer, North talked thickly and with satisfaction around exhaled cigarette smoke. "But my objective would be to use—let me rephrase that—to convince Sarah to get to her son."

"Wouldn't we do better if you stay away? She gets a little testy when you're around."

"Maybe that's to our advantage. You and Pierre can be the good cops, Jen-Jen. We know what role that leaves me."

### CHAPTER 23

North and Constable Pete Heemstra entered Sarah McKinley's barn with Constable Jennifer Duchamps behind them. A heavy outside door slapped shut after Jennifer. A rope ran from the door up through a pulley and down to rusted cultivator parts acting as counter-weights.

"Thought you'd be used to this scene," Pete said, "being a Saskatchewan boy and all."

"We had a store in Kindersley, Pierre. And my friends from the farm—all two of them—came from grain operations. They didn't have to wipe the chitter off their boots when they got inside the town limits." North made an elaborate show of checking the bottoms of his boots, one at a time. They contained nothing more nocuous than straw fragments clinging to packed snow in the treads.

Pete hunched his neck so he wouldn't bump his head against hand-hewn, whitewashed beams supporting a hay mow above. The barn was warmed by the body heat from beige and cream-coloured cows, a sea of them, steam rising from backs or exhaled through wide, wet nostrils, some poking heads through stanchions into a concrete feed trough. Cats scurried about. North sneezed, twice. Dust from a mill grinding corn kernels drifted across the cattle and the manure, adding another layer to a hundred cobwebs on ceiling joists.

At the far end, Sarah was adjusting a lever that controlled the speed of corn silage spilling from a chute to the concrete floor. When she seemed to be satisfied, she hit a large red button, and the unloader quit. She walked over to the corn-grinding mill. With a wide-mouthed aluminum shovel, she pushed yellow cracked corn down an incline into a bin under the mill. She shut down the mill and was moving back toward the silage when she spied the officers. "Look what the cat dragged in and the dog forgot to take back out."

"Good afternoon, Sarah," said Jennifer.

Sarah smirked at her and said, "Travelling with double trouble this time. Give me a minute to finish up."

It took 15 minutes for the woman to run out five wheelbarrow loads of strong-smelling silage and dump them into the manger for the cows, followed by two wheelbarrows of corn scattered atop the silage and three large plastic pails of a brown feed additive from a white bag. Two cats licked at the feed additive. She kicked at them, but they returned to it as soon as she was gone. "That stuff could make them fertile as the old woman who lived in the shoe. It's the hormones. You should give it a try, Jennifer. You and Marcel thinking of reproducing any time soon?"

Jennifer blushed and stammered, "Right now, we're concentrating on our careers."

"The two-income household. Some of us have trouble getting by on one. But I don't suppose you're here to talk about mortgages and kids. Who's this fella?"

Pete stepped forward and extended a hand, bumping his head on an overhead log. "Constable Pete Heemstra."

"Watch yourself. They built these things low years ago, and they're a bitch to modify. Course, people like me and the sergeant, we skinny under them timbers, no problem." She pumped Pete's hand. "Sarah McKinley, but you probably know that."

"I'm part of the team investigating two deaths and an accident that we're treating as suspicious."

"An accident. What turned this into a hat trick?"

"A woman in town," North said. "Somebody we think may have been involved with the Pythons."

"Involved?" Sarah removed a glove, placed thumb and forefinger above her nose and blew once, with force. "You mean, sleeping with them?" She swiped across her nostrils, mucus glinting on the back of her hand, replaced the glove and screwed up her eyes at Jennifer.

"We're not completely sure, Sarah. She was a dancer at the clubs, the one that burned and also the Amber Lee. And now she's in hospital."

"What happened?"

"There's an investigation into that." Jennifer glanced at North. He ignored this and kept his eyes fixed on Sarah.

"Means you don't think it was accidental." Sarah lowered her gloved hands and shunted her overalls back and forth at the waist, as if relieving discomfort in her underclothes. "So this Einstein..." She jabbed a thumb at North. "... He claims this dancer was involved with bikers. And my Duncan rides a Harley. You put two and two together and square it to come up with 10 or 12, depending what time of day it is."

Pete leaned over, picked some stray yellow kernels of corn off the concrete, rolled them in his hand and popped them into his mouth, biting down and chewing. "You can understand why we'd be curious about that relationship. And whether you could help us."

A cow near Jennifer twisted its head from between two vertical pipes and backed up. The animal coughed damply four times, its midriff heaving. Sarah studied the cow. "What do you three stooges have in mind?"

North decided to match her plain talk. "Your son is in a situation he can't control. Inside yourself, I think you know that. We want you to help us."

The cow coughed again. A second, darker animal butted the first one out of the way and stole her place at the feed trough. "I hope there's nothing wrong with that one. They're all bred to come in this March or April. Cattle prices these days, I can't afford to lose any."

"Did you hear what I said?"

Sarah swivelled her head toward Jennifer, lips parted in a smile. "Might be able to hear a whole lot more if there were a couple less of us in the barn."

Jennifer slapped dust off her dark slacks and looked Sarah squarely in the face. "What about you, me and Constable Heemstra? I'm sure Sergeant North wouldn't mind stepping out for a few minutes."

North considered his response and said, "Nobody's leaving. I want to hear this first-hand."

Sarah leaned an elbow against the top of the corn hopper. White insulation poked out from a rip in the grey arm of her jacket. She eyeballed North and smiled. "Suit yourself, I guess. I done business with worse in my day. You're asking me to talk to Duncan."

"It would be a big help," North said.

"That ain't going to happen. You will not find me playing stoolie on my own flesh and blood."

"Two people are dead, one injured. A police officer appears to have committed suicide."

Sarah interrupted him. "I didn't hear about any suicide. People are born, and they die every day, same as cattle. I know it's different with people, but still. These folk you're referring to, I don't know them, any more than I know some poor bugger gets himself blown up in Afghanistan."

Jennifer said softly, "What about Duncan?"

"What about him?"

"He's all you've got left, Sarah, the only one who comes to see you. You must hate the idea that he's riding with the Pythons. You can get him out of that life."

Sarah scanned the barn. Steam rose from piles of fresh green and brown manure. "And how would I manage that miracle?"

"You get him to testify. In return, we offer protection for him and for you."

"It's not in me to turn on my own son." Sarah's gaze rose from the barn floor to a square window, dulled by cobwebs and frosted with patterns. "Or to trick him into testifying against his friends. No matter what they done, that just ain't in my bones to do."

The woman seemed to be pondering something. Taking a leaf from Norval Vandenberg, North adopted a steady, soothing tone. "Okay, Mrs. McKinley. Okay." He stopped and her eyes shifted over to lock on his. "I have children myself. They're younger than yours, and for different reasons, I don't see them very often. Doesn't mean I ever stop caring about them. Or stop wanting what's best for them."

Sarah's eyes moved away. The corners of her mouth drooped. "We all want that. I don't know why I'm sayin' it, because it never happens, but I might have done a few things different. I think about that, but it's too late now."

"It's never too late. We all keep doing what we can." North opened his arms, palms of his leather gloves up in a conciliatory gesture. "Look, I can understand if you don't want to wear a wire. We had that in mind, but that would be asking too much."

"You got that right."

With loud slurps, a cow drank from a metal trough along a wall. An electric motor hummed, filling the trough. Another cow shuffled forward. "Would Duncan come see you if you called him?"

"Always has."

"So let's say you give him a shout. You make sure he's by himself. You figure out some reason it has to be that way. Maybe you have news from your son in Vancouver or you want to talk about the farm, how to handle the inheritance."

"Okay, let's say I get him here. I doubt I have to lie to do it. Then what?"

"Maybe he visits you in the kitchen. We're in the room next door. The door's open a crack, so we can listen."

Sarah's eyes seemed far away, as if she were imagining how such a conversation might go. "I don't need you to get the truth from Duncan."

Pete started to say something, but North waved him away. When nobody replied to Sarah, she turned back to North. "You want him to rat out his friends."

"Do you think his friends are good for him? Are you saying you approve?"

"That might be none of your business. But since you asked, him and me, we don't talk about that no more."

In the straw and dust at her feet, using the toe of her right boot, Jennifer worked semi-circle lines, a miniature rainbow shape. "Maybe it's time to put the subject back on the table."

A dusty black cat arched its tail and back and rubbed against the old woman's wide pant leg. Her face blanched as she glanced from one police officer to the other. "The way things are now, at least he's alive. I get to see him once in a blue moon. You've seen what happens to people that goes up against the Pythons. And that asshole, Turk."

"We've seen it in spades." Pete said.

North studied the pattern Jennifer had made. A rainbow. Hope seemed to be a rare commodity these days. His daughter had been wearing a tan

T-shirt the last time he'd seen her, with the words "Since I gave up HOPE, I feel a lot better" stretched across her breasts. And when had she developed breasts? North shook his head, coughed into his hand and said, "We're offering protection, to Duncan and to you. I think we both know the noose around Turk is tightening. There's three deaths, if you want to include a police officer who killed himself. We think his death may be tied to the Pythons."

Sarah raised her eyebrows. Her thin lower lip rose to cover the upper one, cracked and chapped by weather. She ran her tongue over the crust of it and sighed.

Jennifer urged her, "Call your son. We're running out of time."

She looked at the backs of cows, her eyes roaming from beast to beast. She didn't say no.

**CHAPTER 24**

Duncan McKinley's laugh was strained and high-pitched. Peculiar, because the red-haired biker was saying something not in the least funny, "So you got the chores all done, Ma? You get at them early in the winter, doncha?"

"Finished up by 5:30. There's a two-year-old heifer I'm keeping an eye on. Breathing trouble, and I can't be sure if it's feed-related or something worse."

A chair scraped the wooden floor. A cup banged the table. "Just shove any of them papers out of your way. Lord knows why I still take the *Times-Journal*. Guess I need somethin' for Bernard's cage. Bernard want a cracker?"

"Cracker." Squawk, squawk. "Cracker."

"Bernard must be about a hundred."

"Older'n Christ himself. So what you been up to since Christmas?" A second chair moved and bumped the hardwood floor.

"Same old, same old." This was followed by another quick burst of high-pitched laughter.

"Guess I don't want to know how you make a living."

"A bit of this, a bit of that." A chuckle was followed by a snort. "I'm an entrepreneur."

"And that rhymes with manure. Which is another way of saying, I think you're full of shit."

"Is that any way to talk to your favourite son?"

"My favourite son." Sarah hooted a laugh and slurped a drink. "Been quiet out here since Hughie passed. His mind was going, but he knew farming, and he was living close. Too many city people cluttering up the landscape."

"He was old, Ma. He was one old fart by the time he died. You told me yourself, the old fucker had a stroke."

"Fucker. Fucker." Squawk, squawk.

"Shut it, Bernard, or you get the hood. There's some things I wish you'd never taught him."

Duncan hooted another fake laugh. "We had some good times. All of us, while I was growing up."

"Those days are gone. I'm not getting any younger."

"Ah, Ma, you'll live forever."

A long pause was eventually broken by Sarah. "Nothin' lasts forever. I don't know what I'm supposed to do with the farm. You ever consider changin' your mind about comin' back?"

A chair bumped. Footsteps sounded, paused and sounded again. A chair moved. A match was struck. The warm smell of cigarette smoke permeated the kitchen, easing through the door, open a crack. "Showin' me how to farm is about as useful as teachin' a nun to have sex."

"Don't start, Bernard."

The parrot's hoarse, cheerful voice sounded. "Sex. Sex."

"So your mind's made up. For sure, you're never going to farm? There's nothin' could persuade you?"

"Them cows would starve, waiting for me to show up twice a day. You love that shit, but it bores the hell out of me."

Sarah's tone became sharper. "I hear there's certain crops you don't mind handling."

Jennifer and North were side-by-side on dining room chairs. North risked opening the door from the den to the kitchen half an inch wider. He could see the back of Duncan's sweatshirt, the width of his shoulders, as the man said, "What are you driving at?"

"I hear you been distributing marijuana."

"Who you been talking to?"

"It ain't like I don't read the papers. I know what bikers get up to."

Duncan squealed out another laugh. "Riding a Harley don't make me a biker, Ma."

"You wear the colours. You come here with other gang members before Christmas. You can kid your own self if you want to but don't lie to your mother."

"Okay, let's say I do ride with the Pythons. So what?"

"The police was here."

"We know. What did they want?"

Nobody said anything for a while, then Sarah asked, loudly, "*We* know?"

Duncan's voice carried a threatening undertone as he quietly rephrased his question. "What did they say they was after?"

"Snooping around about the fire. It was me called it in. I seen two snowmobiles over there that night, New Year's Eve. Two guys was dropping something off. I heard this pop, like a firecracker, just the once. Later on, other noises. I'd say they was shots, from inside the house. The snowmobiles left right after the fire started."

"You told the cops all that?" The question came out muffled around exhaled cigarette smoke.

"Are you saying there was something I should've been covering up?"

"They didn't ask no questions about me?"

"This female cop, Jennifer, she mentioned you. She was a McKillop. Her dad had turkeys on the fourth concession, before he went broke at them. You remember her?"

"When she was a little girl, that's all."

"She remembers you. She's with the St. Thomas police. Married a French guy, this Marcel Duchamps."

A lighter flint scraped, and Duncan drew in on another smoke. "You got anything strong to drink, Ma?"

"Haven't had time to restock since your buddies was here. Down to coffee."

"I could take another coffee."

A pot clinked. Coffee was poured. A refrigerator door opened and closed. A spoon tinkled against a cup. Duncan said, "This Jennifer say anything else?"

"Not much. Just asking about you."

"What exactly did she say?"

Sarah's voice was lower. "That you were known to the police. Whatever that means. Are you?"

"Anything else?"

"To say hi, if I saw you, and to ask you to not leave town any time soon."

"Son of a bitch. Fucking son of a fucking bitch."

The bird parroted him, twice. The man stood. His boots thudded around the kitchen floor. A rattling noise came from the direction of the cage. "We had enough out of you." He resumed his seat and asked, "That all she said?"

"That's about it."

"There's a guy she runs with on the force we don't like much."

"I bet I know the man, name of North. A regulation Grade A arsehole."

From behind the door, North poked Jennifer in the ribs. He clamped a hand over his mouth and held his breath to muffle a smirk before it turned into laughter.

"You said on the phone you wanted to talk about the farm." Duncan ingested coffee and inhaled cigarette smoke. "You're asking about me coming back. But we know the answer to that one. So what's next for you? You thinking about selling? Moving to town?"

"I'd rather die in my boots than spend half a day in an apartment. But still..."

"Still what, Ma?"

"We don't always get to choose. I found a lump."

"Jeez, what are you saying?"

With rising irritation, she repeated herself, "I found a lump." And added, "My left boob."

"You been to the doctor? Going for treatments?"

Sarah sounded as gentle as North had ever heard her, gentle and wistful. "Me and doctors get along about as good as you and cattle."

"That mean you've got another plan?"

"I'd like to make one. Maybe there's some other way you could come live here. I'd sell the cattle, what the hell? We'd take the cash from that, and we'd make more by renting out the land. You ain't married. We could live off that."

A black cat curved its shining back and tail as it rubbed against Duncan's leg. He kicked it away. "You don't understand."

Her voice stayed soft. "Tell me what I don't understand." North couldn't tell for sure, but he thought he saw her hand move to Duncan's sleeve.

Duncan's voice was thick with distress. "I'd rather die from the big C than go up against Turk. Once you're in, you're in, Ma. There's no resignin' and comin' back to the farm."

"You wouldn't have to farm it. We could rent out the land. After I'm gone, you could set up an operation here, get your own crew. You wouldn't be run by a man like Turk."

Duncan shouted, "Jesus, Ma. We don't truck chickens for a living. We're not delivering fuel around Elgin." He stopped and lowered his voice. "Let me tell you something, and we could both die if this gets out. I was on one of those snowmobiles New Year's Eve."

"At Hughie's place? You was there?"

"We were dropping something off."

"What are you telling me?"

"The silo was empty. I knew Hughie wasn't right in the head. He'd never know what was going on. We needed temporary storage."

"Were you dropping off drugs?"

"Worse than that."

Sarah sounded defeated. "Something you had to get rid of?"

"It wasn't supposed to go down like it did. Nobody was going to get hurt. It was a natural gas fire. Late at night, nobody there. We was just looking after business."

Sarah's voice was stronger but still neutral, as she said, "Sometimes you gotta do these things."

"Problem was, some idiot was sleeping in one of the old rooms upstairs. He comes barrelling out the window in a ball of fire and breaks his neck."

"So you couldn't leave him there."

"It's one thing to maybe deal with arson. It's another thing to have a dead guy. We had to get rid of him. Me and this other guy, we looked after it."

"You took the body to Hughie's old silo? You and this other guy?"

"One hell of a night, freezing cold. We brought him out on the Skidoos. Hughie, the old bastard, goes nuts. Shoots at us. Somethin' crazy goin' on in his mind. "

"You're not telling me you killed Hughie. And burned his place down."

"I wouldn't kill old Hughie."

"So it was that other guy, the guy you was with? Was it Turk?"

"I ain't sayin' another goddamn word about that. But surely to Christ you can see, you're either in or you're out. And there's only one way out I know of."

"What about prison? At least you'd be safe there."

"Ha. That's one of your best lines ever, Ma."

A kitchen clock bonged the hour. Nobody said anything for a while. Duncan asked her again about the lump, how big it was, when she had first noticed it. He encouraged his mother to go to Emergency.

Sarah said that wasn't going to happen. "We're both in one hell of a pickle, ain't we, Duncan?"

"Maybe you are, Ma. Me, I got no pickle. It's just one foot in front of the other. You make your bed, and you lies in it, even if it's full of shit half the time. Better than the alternative."

"What alternative is that?"

"Forget I said that. You're makin' out like this is all doom and gloom, when it ain't. We got a huge shipment coming through Cornwall. Sweetest deal ever. We're going to be millionaires. When I get my share, I'll fly you to the States for one of them bang-up cancer treatments."

"Cornwall? What you got to do with Cornwall?"

"Nothin'. It's a place to bring stuff in."

"Don't say another word, Duncan. Not one word."

"What are you talking about?"

"I can't get old Hughie off my mind. He wasn't bothering nobody."

"You don't understand."

"Shut up, Duncan."

A chair was pushed back. Stocking feet crossed the kitchen floor. Sarah's wide frame blocked out the light. She flung the door to the dining room open, almost striking North's nose.

"Come out, come out, wherever you are."

### CHAPTER 25

North blinked twice and gave Sarah McKinley a wild look. He stood, brushed past her and strode into the kitchen, reaching for his weapon. Behind him, Jennifer banged her knee against the chair North had been using. She swore softly and limped after North. She bent over to rub the knee, before leaning against the kitchen wall behind him.

"The fuck, Ma?" Duncan scrambled to his feet, patting his belt, checking for a weapon and finding none. Arms rising, fists clenched, he swivelled toward North.

"This conversation was starting to get interesting. Why don't you have a seat?"

Duncan looked like he'd just been hit. "Ma, you didn't." He glanced at North's piece, turned back to his chair and sat. He slumped there. His red beard, flecked with grey, was in the palms of his hands. His fingers massaged the flesh of his face up and down, its pallor alternating between a flushed red and white.

Sarah said, "It's not just because of Hughie." She put a hand on his shoulder. He shook it off, so she left him.

"What else do you think it's about?"

"These people are the only chance you got, Duncan."

Duncan stared at the wallpaper opposite him, blistering near the ceiling—teapots and flowers on a pale yellow background. "Seems like the perfect way to get us both killed."

"They're offering protection."

Duncan emitted one of his high-pitched laughs at the wallpaper. He glanced at his mother before his eyes settled on North, who sat at the end of the table near the door. Jennifer was behind Duncan. Sarah returned to a larger chair with armrests at the end of the table, opposite North.

Duncan said, "Protection? That's what they told you, Ma? Like they protected Candy and that jerk-off police officer who ate his own gun? That the future you envision for me?"

"Your chances ain't great either way. But they seem better if you turn yourself in. Least you'll be alive."

Flicking open a Zippo lighter, Duncan ignited a Player's plain with trembling fingers and blew smoke at the ceiling. "I'm not blaming you, Ma. You always had good intentions."

"More than just the intentions. I can see a way out, for you."

"That's exactly why we came to your mother, and now we're talking to you. Her ways may be a little unorthodox." North glared at the old woman. "But she has your interests at heart. As do we. We'll do everything in our power to ensure your safety."

"Ma, you'll never see me again. You'll go through this cancer thing alone. That dream of me living here and renting the farm, maybe running my own crew—even if I think whole idea is mostly bullshit—that's all gone."

"They'll put you in a protection program."

"They'll relocate me to Hogwash, Manitoba. I'll be cleaning toilets in some school. That's until the Pythons find me. There's a chapter in Winnipeg. You'll never hear how they did me, but it won't be pretty."

"I'm not in bed with these people, particularly not this one." She forked a thumb in North's direction. "But it's your best shot at staying alive. And out of jail. People like us, we can't stand to be penned in."

For a while, nobody said anything. Duncan appeared to be thinking. Jennifer moved away from the wall and took a chair across from him. She slid a pile of newspapers out of her way, toward Sarah, who was studying the grain in the wood of the table as if it might tell her something. Jennifer's tone was quiet and even. "I remember you from when I was a kid, Duncan. I'm with your mother on this. You're not a bad guy; you're just running with a bad crowd. There has to be a way out. Haven't you been thinking the same?"

Duncan's mouth twisted. His beard vibrated from the effort of holding back his emotions. His gaze shifted to his mother—who continued to peruse the table top—and back up to the wallpaper.

"We heard you tonight," North said. "You were at Campbell's place the night he was killed, and you dropped off a body. You are an accessory to Campbell's murder, and you're linked with the death of the other man. Plus, indignity to a body, the way you tried to dispose of it. If we go to court, you'll get 10 to 15. For each death."

"Or I serve them concurrent. And with good behaviour, I'm out in five to seven. Or maybe my lawyer plea-bargains. I get less, and after three or so of good behaviour, I'm a free man."

"You also confessed to what sounded like drug-running through Cornwall. That could give you a whole other stretch."

"I confessed to nothin'. Nobody's read me my rights."

"We have two witnesses to what you said. Three, if your mother testifies. So here's the alternative, and you should be taking it. You cooperate with us, we develop an agreement with the RCMP, and you enter Witness Protection. And you ride away on your Harley."

"You don't have any of this set up, that's what you're telling me? You still got to approach the RCMP and *see* whether they'll do this deal?"

"Strictly speaking, yes. But biker gangs are almost as important to them as terrorists. We should have approval by Monday. Sooner if I make wheels turn over the weekend."

Duncan's eyes moved to regard North's, and North glimpsed a calculating gleam. "Federal civil servants? Not too damned likely. Let's say I do this. I get, what, exactly?"

"A new location, a new identity, financial assistance to make the transition, things like that."

"The idea you'd never see your mother again is just so lame." Jennifer leaned toward Duncan, her expression pleasant, friendly, not in the least threatening. "For your own safety, you would want to stay away for at least a few months. After that..."

"A few months. How long you think you got, Ma, with the cancer?"

Jennifer answered him. "Thousands of women discover a lump every day. Nobody knows it's cancerous, not yet. With early detection..."

Duncan cut her off. "I got to assume you heard what Ma had to say about doctors and treatment, since you was snoopin' in on everything else. You ain't one for hospitals, is you, Ma?"

Sarah looked from one officer to the other, then at Duncan. She made a face and shook her head.

"Plus, I got to testify. That's the part you people seem to be missing. It's me in the witness box, not any of you. So this ain't just about keeping me alive, which I have my own reasons to doubt you can do. It's also about givin' up your best friends. Would you squeal on the people you work with?"

"If they were running drugs and killing innocent old farmers, I would not hesitate," North said. "We're not talking parking violations."

"Blah, blah, blah," said Duncan.

"Look, I understand this whole biker gig looked like a lot of fun when you started out. You got to ride your Harley, move a little dope and get laid by the occasional hooker. But look at yourself now. Where did this 'Ride Free Or Die' shit get you?"

"I don't care what this jerk thinks, but I want you and Ma to understand." Duncan studied Jennifer's face, as if to confirm that she was on side with him. "It made a difference when I heard Ma might be sick. I'm not Turk, and I never will be. I done some bad things, but at least I think about them sometimes."

"I know you'd like to get out. Your mother knows it, too. That's why she agreed to talk to you and let us listen in."

"That will bother me till I die. But you believed you was looking out for me, right, Ma?" His tone became more cynical as he said, "Or was she tricked by you? I suspect it was a bit of both. Okay, since we're talking anyway, if there's a next step, what might that be?"

"We take you into town," North said. "We get a statement, and then we get ahold of the RCMP and put a protection program in place. Until that's done, we secure you in a cell in St. Thomas or more likely, the detention centre in London."

"It's over, right now, if I say yes?"

Jennifer and North nodded almost simultaneously.

The old woman's voice at the end of the table rumbled in a tired way. "I'm not sure how much time I got, Duncan."

"I got to think about this, eh?" Duncan stood suddenly. "You can't decide something this important in 30 seconds."

North was on his feet. "What's there to think about?"

"Everything."

"Maybe we should arrest you right now."

"Maybe you should screw a Holstein." Duncan was breathing heavily, his chest heaving. "You want to arrest me, arrest me. Course, that'd be the end of any talk about the protection program."

"You're saying you can't decide in 30 seconds." North allowed his voice to rise, as if he had enough of Duncan McKinley. "How much time does a man of your intelligence need to make a decision?"

"As much as it takes, you fuckin' prick." Duncan circled his chair. "I can't believe you brought Ma into this."

"That's not acceptable."

"Okay, accept this." Duncan moved fast for a man carrying extra weight. He took one step left, grabbed the back of his chair, and heaved it shoulder-high at North's head. North ducked, his arms coming up instinctively to protect his face as he moved left. The chair came at him sideways, striking his right forearm and the side of his head. He groaned and rolled toward the kitchen wall.

Jennifer stood and reached for her gun. Sarah was out of her chair. She seized Jennifer's arms and spun the female officer toward her like a young calf. "What the hell?" Jennifer struggled in the old woman's grasp.

"Move." Sarah puffed out the words to her son, her chest heaving. "Get out of here. I can't hold her forever."

Duncan dropped the chair and took three steps behind North. He snatched his winter jacket off a rack by the front door. The exterior door slammed. Within seconds, the snowmobile engine roared, followed by a whine as it sped away.

CHAPTER 26

North woke in his hotel room at 11:13 a.m. His upper body was sore, his neck stiff. He'd spent three hours the night before in the St. Thomas Elgin General Hospital. His right forearm, badly cracked, was in a cast. He had a lump on the left side of his head. The instant he was awake, his mind was flooded with thoughts and images from the previous night.

North sat up and reached for a bottle of Tylenol 3s on the bedside table. He swallowed two tablets with stale water from a plastic glass. He felt old.

What day was this? With his left hand, he rubbed his dark hair. Saturday. Tonight, he was supposed to be in goal for the St. Thomas Jumbos in the over-35 league. Like that was going to happen. It was clumsy work, but he used his cell to dial Stan Zivkovic's number, got his machine and left a message asking him to substitute in goal. Stan was a decent defenseman who lacked the excellent peripheral vision and timing of a good goalie. But there was nobody else.

Getting dressed was awkward. The forearm in the cast was like a club, but he used it to hold his pants against his waist while he buckled and zipped up with his other hand. He pulled a loose sweater over his head by inserting the bad arm through his sleeve first. Tying his shoes required considerable time and some cursing.

He sat at the desk in his room and thought about the day ahead. After Duncan's escape, and once she knew North was looked after at the hospital, Jennifer had roused a disoriented and barely cooperative judge out of bed at 2:00 a.m. She secured two search warrants aimed at Turk's farm property and the Pythons' strip club, seeking Duncan McKinley or indications of his likely whereabouts. Both warrants had been executed before 4:00 a.m. Jennifer had updated North by telephone around 8:00 a.m. No sign of Duncan McKinley at either place. As before, a few weapons, all of them registered. A small quantity of marijuana, not enough to prosecute. Nothing else suspicious.

"Now that an officer has been assaulted, we have more options with the Pythons," North had told Jennifer over the phone.

"We had a lot more options when we had Duncan McKinley," she had said.

"You and I did a fine job of good cop/bad cop."

"Until the end."

North had chuckled, "Maybe I went a little over the top."

"Who knows? I thought you did an awesome job. Next time, I want to play bad cop."

"You don't sound like your usual happy self."

Jennifer's laugh had come low, but North had been encouraged to hear it. "Don't I? I've had better days. Let's see, I've been roughed up by mamma bear. The guy we tried to set up is on the loose. And I've had zero sleep."

North shoved himself off his chair and crossed the carpet to open a dark curtain. A burst of light hurt eyes already aching from too many painkillers and too few hours of sleep. He closed them, yawned, scratched his head and ventured another peek. No wind. Sunlight glinted off white waves, curling from the parking lot to the cornfield to the woods beyond. A perfect Canadian winter scene, if a person was into that. North had spent time in the north, in Nunavut, and hadn't minded it then. Something had changed, leading to this dread of winter. Connie's leaving before Christmas hadn't helped.

Hockey gave him something to do in the dark days and kept him in some semblance of shape. But they hadn't played over the holidays, and with his arm in a cast, he wouldn't be on the ice again any time soon.

He should call his kids.

He should have a coffee.

He needed a shower. However, he wasn't about to attempt undressing and dressing.

A coffee—dripped through a machine in his room, treated with coffee whitener—helped bring him around. A second coffee from the continental breakfast area, with a cigarette—its smoke swirling to join the brilliant light outside the downstairs lobby doors—worked a minor miracle. He was coming around.

Back in his room, North dialled the Burlington number for Maddy and Dylan, who should be up by now. The call had its risks. He could handle talking to his ex-wife, Odd, but he wanted to avoid the new man in her life: the king of carpet cleaners in the Hamilton/Burlington area. Maddy had told North the man was "like getting serious with mom." North thought that Odd getting serious with anybody was about as likely as him drawing a straight flush when somebody else was all-in.

No-one answered the telephone. The answering machine came on. A relief in one way. As his children entered their teen years, North found it increasingly difficult to know what to say to them. But North wasn't prepared for the machine, and his message came out as, "Hi, it's Dad. I, um... I haven't been in touch since Christmas, and I wanted to call and say hi to you guys." (Was "guy" acceptable to Maddy?) "It's Saturday morning, and things happened, so if you call the apartment phone number, I won't be there for while." (Did that sound like he was seeing another woman?) "I... well, it's police business. I love you, Maddy and Dylan. Let's stay in touch." (Time to end this; he was rambling; he'd already mentioned staying in touch).

North left them his cell phone number and said goodbye. He switched on the television, ran through the channels, watched highlights from NHL games from the previous week and turned it off. He pulled out his phone, checked his stored addresses and found the number for Orwell George, an OPP Criminal Investigations Bureau contact from the Brantford area.

Orwell remembered him right away. North thanked him for being one of the few people who had called after the powers-that-be in Belleford had turned against him. He gave Orwell a quick sketch of the investigation into allegations of Tom Skelding's crack cocaine problems.

"I heard something about it internally, and of course, his death has been all over the news," Orwell said. "I'm not personally involved with the Skelding investigation. What's your interest?"

"He's connected with this case I'm working on." North offered Orwell a short outline and ended with, "My opinion... he was a good cop."

"Mainly, you want to know if there was a drug link him between him and the Pythons?"

"That, and one other thing. There's talk that Tom was feeding the Pythons information. That part bothers me as much as the drug issues."

"So what exactly can I do for you?"

"Any chance you could get me an off-the-record update on the Skelding investigation?"

"Give me half an hour."

North watched a syndicated *Seinfeld* episode until his cell rang. Orwell said, "We understand Tom started using crack from a supply at the station. Stuff confiscated in a raid."

"The stupid bastard."

"It gets stupider. He liked it so much, he moved on to the Pythons as a source."

"There's evidence of that?"

"It's building all the time. Look, the guy's dead, so I don't expect this investigation to go on and on."

"Did anybody say, was he ratting us out to bikers?"

"Not sure. My guy says they're still looking. I'll get back to you."

North needed time to absorb what he'd just learned. After a late lunch at the Cozy Corner Café, he stopped by his old apartment. A police officer followed him from the hall into the living room where North checked for messages. Connie had left an inquiry and her telephone number some time before her visit to his hotel room. He deleted that message and listened to another from his daughter Maddy, asking him what was up. He returned this call, got her machine again, and hung up.

Yellow tape criss-crossed his balcony. He nodded to the officer and was about to call the hospital for an update on Candy when his cell phone chirped. "Sergeant Carl North," he said.

"They got my boy." Sarah McKinley's voice cracked and she sobbed. "Oh, Duncan, my son, my boy."

### CHAPTER 27

Steering with his good arm, North risked sliding off snow-packed roads on the two-kilometre drive from the edge of the city of St. Thomas proper to Sarah's farm. He managed to avoid a crash or a plunge into a ditch and made it to Sarah's driveway inside 12 minutes.

He knocked on the front door, shoved it open and called Sarah's name. No answer. He shut the exterior door before a black cat with orange marbling around the throat and face could slither past him. He followed a snow-packed path between drifts to the barn, his shoes slipping on snow and frozen manure. Before driving out, he should have taken the time to change into boots. He moved gingerly ahead and into the barn.

Wearing masculine garb, Sarah McKinley was plopped down on the concrete run above the manger where she fed cows twice daily. Her gloves were off. Her fingers were stroking red hair with grey streaks. The hair was fanned out across her lap. Her overalls were dusty. Face up, eyes closed, legs splayed in a snowmobile suit, Duncan was lying in front of her. Black blood crusted his throat. It had been slashed.

The woman rocked herself back and forth. "I hope it was quick, that's one thing. I believe it was that way."

"I'm sorry. I... "

Back and forth, back and forth, slowly and rhythmically, her head bobbing with this motion, her fingers twisting and curling through the hair. "They did him like a hog."

"That's terrible," North said quietly.

"I haven't done one in years, not since we got out of the pigs."

North didn't know how to respond, so he said, "Now, it's just cattle."

"When you do one, there's blood galore. Terrible amounts of it. It seems to take a while, and you got to hold them tight, to keep them from squirming away, getting into the dirt. They squeal, but it's the fear. There's not a lot of pain. There can't be."

Where are memories stored and what dredges them up? North's mind flashed to his thin mother with her dark, unruly hair. Her last, demented days. He thought he had locked that box for good, but it apparently opened anyway. Inside was darkness and a perfumed, nursing home smell. "I know Duncan meant the world to you."

Straw was intertwined in her son's matted hair. Sarah's lined cheeks glistened with tears. Mucus ran from her nose to her upper lip. "I think they was almost kind, in their own way. That's why they did Duncan like this. Had to make a point, but he wasn't tortured."

Cows milled about in the pen. More were outside, in the sunshine, hooves slipping in the semi-frozen yard. Two cats rubbed against Sarah. One leaped onto Duncan's unmoving chest and licked at dark blood around his neck. Sarah swatted it away. "My Duncan knew what he was talking about. He as much as told us what would happen."

"We won't know, until there's been a thorough investigation." North silently castigated himself for slipping into police jargon. Maybe it didn't matter. Sarah didn't appear to have heard him.

She rummaged two balled-up tissues out of her coat pocket. She swiped at her cheeks and her nose and flung the tissues into the manger. A cow's rough, pink-grey tongue snaked forward and curled around a tissue, bringing it in with a wad of silage. "I should never've opened that door. Should never've let you into my life to start with. But I sure should never've opened that door to the parlour."

"You were doing what you thought was best for Duncan."

"I been thinking a lot about something my dad used to say. Your greatest strength's also your greatest weakness."

Sarah was following her own trail of thoughts. "I've never been afraid to try somethin', send out a trial balloon and see what happens. But with you two, that was one time I should've left well enough alone."

North walked to the door he'd come in, opened it for some air and then closed off the sunlight. "You don't know that, not for sure, nobody does. We pick one way and go with it. Right or wrong, we never know until later."

"I know that. I also know my Duncan's gone, and there ain't a damned thing I can do to bring him back. Not one damned thing."

North's eyes roamed over the shifting backs of cows as he walked back to her. He hunkered down, his left knee bent more than his right, his cast perpendicular across one knee. "There is something you can do."

"What's that?"

"Help us get Turk."

### CHAPTER 28

"You can't take my boy."

"It's time, Ma'am." A female OPP officer North didn't know turned her Smokey-the-bear hat toward him.

Sarah seemed to be searching North for an answer. She looked old. "Do they have to autopsy him?"

North nodded. His arm was sore. It was dark outside the barn windows. Inside, hungry cows were circling, sticking heads through stanchions, coughing and bawling. North was exhausted from the work of the past three hours—it seemed like two days since he'd called in Duncan's death to the St. Thomas police, and they'd contacted the OPP. On top of everything else, it had been tiring work to repeatedly explain that he wasn't investigating anything—Sarah had called him. Even though Duncan's body had been transported to Sarah McKinley's farm, even though this wasn't, strictly speaking, *the* crime scene, it had taken a couple of hours to separate and label every possible piece of evidence, from footprints and tire tracks to what Duncan was wearing and carrying. It all counted in court. And there had to be continuity in how it was handled. Too often, suspects walked on technicalities.

Two ambulance attendants wheeled a gurney down the concrete wheelbarrow run above the cattle. Hay and dust adhered to the black gurney wheels, turning them grey.

North stepped past the ambulance attendants and joined Sarah McKinley and the OPP officer. Sarah looked at him in a distracted way. "I want to bury my boy with dignity. From a church."

"You'll be able to do that."

"I don't want them to cut my Duncan any more."

North placed his left hand on her left arm, over her coat. Sarah seemed to allow that, so he left his hand there. "We'd all feel the same. You'll have him back for a proper funeral in a church, if that's what you want."

"What'll he look like?"

North glanced at the female officer who was staring at Sarah with intense, bright eyes. "He'll look fine." North knew that might be a small lie, but white lies didn't kill anybody. "They won't have to do as much as if the cause of death was unknown." But he knew that if the District Coroner's Office didn't do a complete autopsy, the defense at a trial could make mincemeat out of the alleged cause of death.

"I want to do the right thing."

"We understand. Tell them it's okay to take Duncan."

Sarah fixed her eyes on her son, struggled with her emotions and said, "You're right to take him." Her chest heaved as a long, broken sigh escaped from her. "I got to remember nothing is bringing him back."

Sarah and the OPP officer and North stepped down into the concrete manger. Startled cows quivered and bolted back two or three feet but kept their large wet eyes on the officials. Emergency services personnel operated professionally and respectfully, as they loaded Duncan's body and wheeled it down the runway to the waiting ambulance. Within 15 minutes, the remaining police presence consisted of an OPP cruiser with two officers parked in the lane for overnight vigilance, yellow tape identifying the so-called crime scene, and North.

Cattle were becoming more agitated, butting each other. Occasionally, a cow jumped its front hooves up along the flanks of another cow, riding it for a few seconds.

"I better get at the chores."

"I'm sure one of the neighbours would help. Why don't you call somebody?"

"Rather do it myself." Sarah's mouth twisted, but she did not cry. "I am not looking forward to spending time in that house tonight, but long as a body keeps moving, it'll usually be okay."

"Let me help you with the chores."

"With that arm of yours? And you're hardly dressed for it."

For the next hour, North played at being a farmer. His usable hand, not toughened by manual labour, felt as if it'd be cut through by the handle of a five-gallon pail of concentrate. His biceps—and his forearm in the cast—ached after helping load the fifth wheelbarrow of silage. Other than quick instructions from Sarah when North asked what he could do, or a comment when Sarah spotted him making a mistake, there was no conversation between them. The whir of the silo unloader and the crackling roar of the feed mill made talking all but impossible.

When they had finished, and Sarah was taking one last look over her herd, she said, "I appreciate the company."

"Glad I could help out."

"Can't avoid the house forever. Want to come in for a coffee?"

North had been sweating while he worked in the barn. On the walk to the house, he was instantly chilled. He brushed dust out of his clothing, cleaned his shoes, and was grateful for the warmth of the kitchen when they entered it. Sarah plugged in a kettle. "I need to check the furnace. It's wood and oil; hasn't been tended to lately. Here, stop bothering the man, Marmalade."

She picked up a cat, nestled it in her arms and left by a narrow door. Her footsteps, descending in heavy shoes, sounded hollow. Metallic noises and bumps rose from the basement. A few minutes later, steps advanced back up. She returned with the cat. "Elm was always the best, but we don't have any of that. Been hit twice in my lifetime by the Dutch Elm disease. God, some men don't even know how to work a kettle." Sarah advanced on the counter, with a hint of amusement, unplugged the cord and made instant coffees for the two of them.

"I got no appetite," she said. "But I'm sure you wouldn't mind something."

North was famished. He said that would be good.

Sarah made hamburgers, two for North and, in the end, one for herself.

When he finished, North patted his abdomen. "If you ever quit farming, you could go into the restaurant business."

"Helps that you was so hungry. Also, there's no meat better than what you raise yourself. That was from a three-year-old heifer, broke a hip after calving last spring."

North wanted to talk more about Duncan but didn't know how to begin.

Sarah said, "You headin' back to the city?"

"I can stay a while."

"Got a wife waiting for you?"

"I'm separated. Well, divorced once, and separated from my second wife. It's complicated."

Sarah seemed to consider this but did not pursue it. "You mentioned kids before."

"A boy and a girl from the first marriage."

"You stay in touch with them?"

"I do what I can."

"It's important. How old are they?"

"Teenagers."

"You're some older than you look. Or else you started young."

Sarah had allowed a second coffee to cool and now drank half of it in two gulps. "I guess you and Duncan to be about the same age." A painful look crossed her face and she added, "If he was still with us, is what I mean."

"Yeah," North said.

"I see on the TV where these people like Oprah and Doctor Phil, they seem to think you have to tell your kids you love them all the time. I don't say they're wrong, but you don't want to spoil 'em. More important to show you love 'em."

"I try to do a little of both."

"M-m-m-m." Sarah finished her coffee in one draught. "My sweet tooth is acting up. You want something?"

They had sticky buns. North's mind was dulled by the food and too much fresh air in the afternoon. When Sarah said, "I been thinkin' about somethin'," he shook himself and said, "What?"

"What you said about Turk. You're pretty sure he murdered my Duncan."

North nodded. "I'm about 110 percent on that."

"So arrest him."

"We've got enough to bring him in for questioning. But he's got the resources to get himself lawyered up in a hurry. It would be a whole lot better if we had more evidence."

"In the barn, you said I could help you." Sarah looked at him steadily. "You have something in mind?"

"That shipment coming in this weekend from Cornwall?"

Sarah looked away, at the newspapers on the table and the cats on the floor. "Well?" she said.

"Do you know anything about it?"

"No. Wait, maybe I do."

"What can you tell me?"

"Might be nothing. One time when Turk was here, Duncan had a skinful in him. He starts talking about needing a church key to open a beer. Next thing I know, he's talking about picking up stuff at a church."

"He say which one?"

"Turk told him to close his mouth and keep it shut. Things was tense for a while."

"There seem to be about 50 churches in St. Thomas."

"And a ton more across Elgin. How do you know it's not one of the country congregations?"

North said, "Okay, but maybe that helps, this church thing. He say anything about the time of delivery?"

"No, well, maybe. When I asked Duncan to come out here, he said he couldn't do it Sunday. Had to be today or Monday."

"Okay, did he say anything else about that?"

"He gave me that laugh of his and said he had to go to church on Sunday."

"But you think he was referring to a shipment coming in tomorrow?"

Sarah nodded. "He wasn't one to darken a church door. Never since he was a kid and I used to make him."

### CHAPTER 29

In deep blue, descending darkness, North idled his unmarked Crown Vic in Sarah's laneway. Two curious cats tripped carefully along ruts and leaped onto his hood. Exploring the surface, they left rounded prints, before curling into balls near the windshield in the warmth rising from the engine. He popped two extra-strength Tylenols to help with the pain in his arm, chasing them with coffee from a cup Sarah had loaned him.

North punched in numbers for the station and asked for Dexter Phillips. When he had Dexter on the line, he said, "Why are you working on a Saturday night?"

"Might as well. I can't dance. What's on your mind?"

"I'm at the Sarah McKinley farm. You heard about her son, Duncan?"

"That might have something to do with me still being here."

North said, "Gotcha. You know how you're always going on about being such a contribution to multiculturalism around the department?"

Dexter chuckled and said, "Somebody has to be the token Indian."

"Want to put your Native heritage to use?"

"In what way?"

"You have any contacts with the police at the Cornwall reserve?"

"I know people with the Akwesasne Mohawk Police. You want cheap smokes? I can probably arrange that."

"Oneida or Muncey are a lot closer and just as cheap. I was thinking about something besides my occasional nicotine addiction. We have reason to believe there's a major drug shipment coming across the beautiful St. Lawrence River."

"And you believe this is through Akwesasne?"

"Yes."

"What kind of drugs we talking?"

"Probably nose candy, from Mexico to Texas, up through the States and across the river into Canada."

"Freeze-up is late coming this year, so they'll still be using boats between islands. Let me see what I can find out. You know when this bonanza is expected?"

"Our initial information was this weekend. We have reason to believe that means tomorrow."

"Thanks for the lead time."

"Anything you can get would be helpful. You have my cell."

North called the St. Thomas Elgin General Hospital. Ivana Genska was still in the Intensive Care Unit. His call was forwarded to the desk on the unit. He asked whether she was allowed visitors.

"We restrict ICU visitors to one at a time. Usually close relatives."

The snow meant that nights never became completely dark. Driving back to St. Thomas felt like crossing a lunar landscape. With the heater on and two Tylenols in his system, he drifted into sleep. To stay alert, he turned down the heat and opened a window. Cold air sang past his left ear. He closed the window, lit a cigarette and opened it again to let the smoke stream out.

The hospital parking lot was humped with snow and white-mounded vehicles. North entered by the east door, following a long corridor to the elevators. Parts of the building had been completely refurbished. Other areas were like a do-it-yourself project the owner never found the time or money to finish. Some walls needed paint, others appeared to have been bunted by equipment and never repaired.

North left the elevator and made his way toward Intensive Care. He kept a firm pace as he passed a nursing station, as if he knew exactly where he was going, and picked up a phone to be buzzed into the unit. A uniformed police officer guarding Candy's room was trying to stay awake on a chair in the corridor. He stood at North's approach. North showed him the badge on his belt and asked how his shift was going.

"Fine, Sir."

"No big-ass bikers showing up? No threats?"

"No, Sir, nothing like that."

North entered a room with a white bed raised at one end. A cast covered her torso, another encased her left arm and a third, her elevated left leg. Her neck was braced. At first, North thought she was unconscious, but she stirred as he entered. Dull eyes tracked his movements.

Her voice croaked, "Mr. Cop Man."

"Hello, Ivana. How you doing?"

"M-m-m-m, wish I was dead."

"Are you in a lot of pain?"

"Drug looks after. I do not think Candy dance again."

North surveyed the white smooth plaster over much of her body. Monitors on a shelf were regularly reporting her pulse and blood pressure. "You don't know that. It's early days still. For what it's worth, I am sorry."

"Both, we are sorry. You and me."

"When I saw you on that chair. Everything happened too fast."

Her head moved slowly side to side. "Not your fault." Her low voice was close to a whisper. "This hospital, how do I pay?"

"Do you have a health card?"

"Yes, but they keep card."

"We'll deal with that later. Right now, you have to focus on the important things. Like getting better."

Her eyebrows rose. "If I do not pay, they send me back."

"Is that so bad?"

A tube had been inserted in one wrist. Another wormed out the back of her body and down the side of the bed. Candy's dry lips parted. "Yes, bad." Her eyes closed. North thought he had lost her to a medicated sleep. They flickered open, and she said, "You are my visitor. Only one"

"It's more than a social call. I want you to help me."

"Please, can you give water?"

North carried a plastic glass to a tiny bathroom with silver-coloured faucets and filled it. She sucked through a straw. Some water dribbled from her lips, onto the top of her cast. North found a napkin to wipe the cast and her chin. Her voice was stronger. "Thank you. Is better."

"You know who did this, right?

"Maybe, maybe not."

"Somebody duct-taped you to the chair and left you on the balcony in the freezing cold. The same guy called me and told me I had a surprise waiting for me back at my apartment."

She moved her good hand to his wrist and applied minor pressure. She shook her head and looked away. "Do you know who broked your arm?"

"Yes, I do."

She removed her hand. "What happen to him?"

North's mind flashed to Duncan, his throat cut, cradled in his grieving mother's lap in a barn with cattle and cats. He decided not to answer that question. "You know who left you on my balcony, don't you? You need to tell me."

Candy refused to look at him.

"Are you willing to say it wasn't me? We both know I opened the patio door, but will you testify that I didn't set you up?"

"This, I tell police. They do not believe."

"They think I tried to kill you?"

"They tell me, if I do not know who does this, how can I say is not you?"

North considered this logic. "I know those guys. I work with them. They're blowing smoke."

"Please, more water."

North accommodated her request. She said, "Thank you and please to raise my bed."

"Let's say it's too dangerous for you to identify these men." North pressed buttons on a remote control that elevated the head of the bed. "I'm glad there's an officer outside your door. Maybe there's another way we can get these guys and keep you safe."

Candy sounded worn out as she said, "What is that?"

"There's a shipment coming in this weekend. Drugs. Did you hear anything about that?"

Candy's eyes moved to take in one side of the room, then the other.

North placed his left hand over hers. "I understand why you are afraid. But even small things can be helpful."

"Everything, they do by cell phone. Turk, he have this drug all over the place. Is better that way. No one place for police to find."

"Was a church one of those places?"

"Is on the street."

Despite his good intentions, North sounded annoyed as he said, "What do you mean? Is on the street?"

Her eyebrows lifted briefly. North had the impression that if she weren't encased in plaster, she would have shrugged. "They say Church Street. Some house on Church Street."

North told Candy he had to go. He left her, and was saying goodbye to the officer outside her door, when a call came in from Orwell George. "Our guys found interesting paperwork at Tom Skelding's home. You were partly right about him."

"How's that?"

"When it came to writing, the guy was cryptic, to say the least, but thorough. He logged phone calls, times, dates, who he talked to, brief notes about what was said. All recorded in a day planner in his desk."

North dodged a nurse running toward the ICU desk as Orwell continued, "None of this exactly negates the drug thing, but we think Skelding wanted to cut his ties with the bikers."

"That fits. Your people find supporting documentation?"

"In Skelding's notes. Looks like Turk responded by threatening Skelding, his wife, his kids. Reminded him of how much money he owed."

North was at the elevators. "How bad did that get?"

"Thirty to 50 thousand. We're still pulling the pieces together."

"Turk put that much on this tab?"

"Ah, yes, but Turk knew what he was doing. To settle the bill, he tried to get Skelding to give him confidential information from inside the force."

"Did Tom follow through?" North pushed the elevator button repeatedly, trying to hurry it along.

"No, but it gets worse. They had Skelding on video, doing crack upstairs at the Amber Lee. When Skelding refused to cooperate, Turk said he'd spread the rumour he was a rat. Too much for Skelding. You know the rest."

## CHAPTER 30

As North was walking past a cluster of wheelchairs, his cell phone rang again. He was nearing the exit door to the parking lot. With his left hand, he fumbled for the phone, simultaneously raising the arm in the cast, as if it could assist him. The number on display seemed familiar. The man's voice was rough. "We know where your kids are."

North had continued walking as he took the call. He stopped. He was inside the hospital, but he felt cold, as if somebody had opened an exit door, and a freezing east wind were sweeping up his pant legs and under his arms. "Who is this?"

The deep voice with the slight lisp sounded pleased about something. "That's for me to know and you to find out. We located your ex. Wasn't hard."

"What are you telling me?"

"A good old Saskatchewan boy like you should be able to put two and two together."

"Are you threatening my family?"

"What should a guy do in this circumstance? I think I know." The voice hardened as the man said, "It's time to back off. Go to your little hotel room for a few days and watch TV."

"And if I don't?"

"Remember Candy?"

The call ended. North dialled the station for confirmation of the number. A cell phone in the Brantford area. From his unmarked car, he called the home of the Hamilton/Burlington carpet king. Maddy answered. North said he wanted to talk to her mom.

Maddy spoke slowly, sounding amused. "She's gone out."

"You mean to the store? Or for the evening?"

"They went to some like stupid ballroom dance or something. She had like this orange ball gown, like she was some princess."

"Can you reach her?"

Maddy enunciated each word distinctly as she answered, "Took her cell phone."

"Call her, and have her call me right away."

"You're being all like Mr. Weird Cop Dad."

"Are you stoned?"

Maddy giggled. "Smoked a little weed. Something wrong with that?"

Anger rose inside North like heat. He took a deep breath, filling his chest and his abdomen before saying, "Make sure you call her, okay? Have her call me right away. On my cell. Is there somewhere you and Dylan can go?"

"Plans, later. Friends coming over. Dyl's got, like his drums. Fooling around on them now."

"When are your friends coming?"

"Soon."

"Did Dylan smoke up as well?"

"Maybe you should ask him."

North didn't relish that thought. "Keep the doors locked, okay? And have your mother call me. I love you."

"You, too. Later, Dad."

North called the number for Connie's parents in Belleford. Her father answered, his voice deep and quavering. North asked for Connie. Her father said she'd gone out.

"Have her call me as soon as you hear from her. Does she have her cell with her? Can you reach her?"

"I'm not certain. Where's the fire, Carl?"

Before the separation, Connie's father had seemed to like North. Maybe he still respected him. North said, "Something's come up that concerns me."

"Has Con done something?"

"It's not that."

"Did you do something? Again?"

Family. There had been no trial, but North was guilty. He said, "I have a concern for her safety. Try to reach her. Have her call my cell. She's got the number."

He rang off. There was a message from Odd, his ex-wife.

He called her, and she answered in a hushed, hurried tone, "Why do you always have to screw things up?"

Music in the background, people chattering, muted laughter. "Can you drive home right away? We need to get the kids out of the house."

"God, Carl, you can be so fucking dramatic. Is it about to blow up or something?"

"You're close. Can you move them to friends, or better yet, a hotel?"

"Your timing is terrible. We're at the reception for the most important art show in this area."

"When did you start caring about art?"

"Hamish knows these things. He says the art world is like business. You have to mingle to get ahead."

North said, "So you're at a gallery?"

"We happen to be at the Casablanca Winery Inn."

"Does it have rooms?"

"We have a suite for the night."

"I want you to go home, get the kids and keep them with you overnight."

"They're not babies, Carl. They've got plans."

North counted to three, thought about what he knew about Odd's past, and said, "Keep this to yourself. But we have a major investigation into a biker gang happening. They've threatened Connie and the kids."

Odd said nothing, and then, like a frustrated adolescent, she said, "What the hell have you done now?"

"What's that supposed to mean?"

"You're positive these are bikers."

"They're not seniors on Gold Wings."

Clapping and laughter erupted in the background of the call. "And they threatened the kids. You're sure?"

"Would I joke about that?"

"Okay, I'll talk to Hamish. He'll figure out how to handle the kids. He can be very persuasive."

"Can you keep them out of the house for a couple of days?"

Traces of her old cynicism permeated her tone. "Whatever you say."

"I'll call you."

There was a message from Connie. North had a similar conversation with her, but she panicked as soon as he asked her to leave her parents' house. She began to hyper-ventilate. He used calming words, and after a time her breathing improved. They agreed her parents should get out with her. Until things settled down, Connie should call in sick at work.

"What about you?" she asked. "I'll be so worried."

"I'll be all right."

North sat in the vehicle with the engine running, more concerned about staying warm than about the environment. Possible next steps raced through his mind. His exes and his children might be safe for a while. But he had to do something, right away, about Turk and the Pythons.

Dexter Phillips answered his cell phone with, "It's your nickel."

North said, "You were going to call me if you heard anything from Akwesasne."

"My sources indicate there could be a movement tomorrow. A big shipment of cocaine coming our way."

"Any details?"

Dexter said, "May be a cube van, expected during daylight hours."

"Must be six or seven hours to St. Thomas. Could be here mid-afternoon. Do you know where it's going? To the farm, maybe?"

"I think the farm's too hot right now. You want to set up something, try to catch the van coming off the 401?"

North said, "Maybe, but there are at least three exits we'd have to cover, more if they decide to get off earlier and come across on Highway 2 or 3. There's another problem. If your information's good, we'd have the drugs but nothing on Turk."

"What else you have in mind?"

"We need to get more on this end. You working tomorrow?"

"I can be."

## CHAPTER 31

North's mind worked best when he was in motion. He nosed the Crown Victoria slowly around parked vehicles and snow mounds, paid five dollars, and exited the hospital lot. He turned left on Elm Street. Here and there, residences displayed Christmas decorations, sad attempts to prolong the Christmas spirit.

The parking lot for the Tim Hortons at the corner of Elm and Wilson was brightly lit and inviting. North pulled into the bumpy, ice-covered lot and rang Sarah McKinley.

She answered on the third ring. He identified himself, and she said, "Oh, it's you."

North tried to inject sympathy into his voice. "How are you doing?"

"Not getting any better."

"These things take a while."

"Maybe a lifetime. And at my age, that ain't so long. I bet you're not calling to talk about me."

A Smart Car zipped into a parking spot across from North. A middle-aged woman with sensible hair exited it. North said, "Something fairly big is going down with the Pythons. We think, tomorrow. Is there anything you can recall that will help? It could be small, but important."

"Helping you people hasn't worked out too good, so far."

"Let's start with the basics. Where was your son Duncan living?"

A short intake of breath was followed by a long exhalation. This happened once more. North didn't prompt her. The woman sounded shaken as she said, "He stayed at the farm with Turk some of the time. And he had a place in St. Thomas."

North kept his voice level. "Do you know where he stayed in St. Thomas?"

"Some apartment in a house on Omemee."

North said, "We'd like to have a look around it, if we could."

"You getting a warrant?"

"That wouldn't be a problem." A black Dodge Ram rumbled into the parking lot beside North, dwarfing his vehicle, making North feel crowded. "But it is the weekend, and it might not be easy to get one in time. If you could help us look around the apartment, that would be a huge help."

"What's this big thing that's going down?"

After a moment's hesitation, North decided to tell her. "We have information on a drug shipment out of the States, via Cornwall."

"You tryin' to bring down Turk?"

"That's the idea."

Sarah gave him the address on Omemee and said she'd meet him there in about half an hour.

★

Sarah pulled up in a long, rusting Ford pick-up with an extended cab. The house on Omemee was an old frame structure that had sagged and settled into a shape that was no longer square. Its exterior was covered in dingy white aluminum. Sarah waved at North to follow. He got out of the Crown Victoria and tramped along a driveway. The skeletal frame of a muscle car had been set in front of a single-car garage, as if somebody intended to rebuild the classic auto. A low-wattage bulb illuminated a door to the apartment with the number "1" above it.

Sarah pointed at his cast. "Should have handicapped parking for invalids like you."

North didn't answer her.

One of Sarah's keys opened an exterior door with a loose lock. This let them into a covered porch with two locked doors marked A and B. Another key opened the A door, leading into a small kitchen with a dirty sink and no furniture. Sarah scuffed her boots on a bristly mat, and North did the same. The greying white floor tiles were gritty. North struggled with the fingers protruding from his cast and managed to slide a plastic glove on his left hand. Sarah didn't offer to help.

Sarah was wearing barn clothes. Faint straw, dust and manure odours emanated from her as she led him into a 10-by-12 living room. She switched on a big-based lamp taking up most of the top of a brown table with narrow legs. "I'm not sure what you're after." She plopped herself into a brown couch with three cushions. "Have a look around."

North was tempted to say, "Neither am I." Instead, he said, "Thank you."

A bathroom was ahead, to his right. North turned on a light and looked inside. Sink, toilet, shower, none of them any cleaner than the kitchen. He shut off the light, left and opened the door to the left of the bathroom. A double mattress was on the floor. A chair above it held a deck of cards, a half bottle of Jack Daniels, denim clothing and a three-pack of condoms, one sleeve ripped open. Two sleeping bags had been tossed across the mattress. A Confederate flag covered the only window.

North opened a built-in closet with sliding doors. He shone his Maglite on a leather vest with Python colours, three sweatshirts and a pair of black jeans. On the floor, sweat-stained socks poked out of a pair of black boots with silver chains. No AK-47. A shotgun leaned against one corner. A box of shells had been opened on a shelf above the clothes. North touched none of these.

In the living room, Sarah sat like a Buddha on the couch, sausage fingers linked in front of her belly. Her eyes swivelled with little interest to North and back to a framed velvet painting on the opposite wall. A cartoon girl with large doe eyes, a rounded face and naked breasts. The soiled carpet was orange, the walls panelled about three feet up from the floor, the balance of the walls and ceiling painted a pale orange.

North sat in a brown imitation leather chair with wide arms and a cracked seat. Duncan had lived, part of the time, in this depressing, disorganized apartment. Sarah grunted, "You find anything?"

North was about to answer when a telephone on a low stand jangled.

Sarah raised an eyebrow at him. North waved her off. After five rings, the answering machine kicked in, broadcasting her son's voice. "Hey, it's me. Go nuts when you hear the beep."

The female voice was between a whisper and a purr. "Hi Duncan. It's Baby Doll. I'm at the club next weekend. You guys want to do church again? Very sexy last time. You know me, you know my rates, you have my number. Give me a call. If I'm not in, leave me a massage." This was followed by a giggle. "I mean, a message. Bye-bye. Big guy."

Looking at Sarah, North said, "Sorry you had to hear that."

Sarah shrugged. "Nothing there I couldn't have guessed at. It struck me hard when I heard his voice, was all."

North opened a drawer in the desk under the telephone. He pulled out an address book. Baby Doll was listed, a Toronto 416 exchange number. North flipped pages, seeing numbers from London, Windsor and Toronto. One Amber, three Krystals, a Tierra. Near the back of the book, he found two numbers for Turk, one of them in St. Thomas.

He used Duncan's telephone to call the station. Dexter Phillips had nothing more to report from Cornwall. North asked him to run a reverse search on the St. Thomas number for Turk and to call him back.

It seemed like a very long five minutes, sitting in an orange room with Sarah, neither of them speaking. North was conscious of the ache in his arm and swallowed more painkillers with water from the kitchen tap. His phone rang. Dexter gave North an address, matching Turk's St. Thomas telephone number, on Church Street.

North said, "I could kiss you. But why don't you go home and let your wife do that?"

Dexter said, "She would, except the Leafs are playing tonight."

"If they're against the Senators, they don't stand a chance."

"Some people have a very warped sense of reality, Sarge."

North hung up, and Sarah shifted forward on the couch, as if ready to leave. Her lined face was expressionless. "I started to make funeral arrangements," she said.

"That's good." North stood by the chair. He decided to take the address book and tucked it between his cast and his ribs.

"No big surprise, but he did no pre-planning, Duncan, I mean. Why would he?" Her lower lip trembled, and she bit it.

"No reason at all. I guess we should go."

The jangle of Duncan's telephone interrupted any further conversation. North didn't answer. Duncan's voice came on the machine, but the caller left no message. North was preparing to leave when his cell phone rang. As with everything he did these days, he was slow in answering. A rough voice with a minor impediment said, "What the hell you doing at that house?"

CHAPTER 32

North said into the small telephone, "You keep better track of me than either of my exes."

The man chuckled and coughed. "You got balls, I give you that. You got enough balls to rescue your ex?"

North's breathing stopped. For an instant, it was as if the world had frozen. Nothing moved. He had to take a breath. He felt dizzy. He heard Turk say, "Hey, you still there?"

"Yeah."

"Buddies from the K-W area visited your wife."

Fear and anger choked North's throat, making it difficult to say, "You touch her, and it's the end of you."

"Somehow, I don't see it that way."

North breathed deliberately, filling his abdomen. He glanced over. Sarah's eyes were bright and locked on his. She seemed to be transfixed by his cell phone conversation. "I think I know how you see it."

"Well-fed, ain't she? More my style than the super-model types like Candy. I like something to grab hold of."

North had a vision of Connie. His fear and anger switched to a cold rage, and with that coldness came a clearer head. "I think you're bullshitting me."

"She was packing suitcases when we got there. Somebody tell her to take a trip?"

That was a little too convincing. Connie wouldn't go to a hotel for a night without at least three suitcases and the Hermes make-up bag she'd won at a trade show. North couldn't help himself. He said, "What about her parents?"

"Give the Belleford cops a call and send them around. Those old geezers need to go to the bathroom some time. Course with folks that age, you don't know. They might never use the facilities again."

North said, "You degenerate bastard."

"Hey, you know the score. The boys may have some fun with your ex, but that ain't why we got her."

"And why exactly do you have her?"

"We need you to back off. And get the other imitation state troopers to do the same. Just for a couple of days. We might give you back, what's her name? Corny or somethin'?"

"Her name is Connie. She's my wife, and if you..."

North was cut off by, "You don't look after this for us, and the next time you see her, she'll be in a plus-size box. You'll be smelling flowers and listening to hymns."

North flipped shut his phone without answering. He called Connie's parents in Belleford. The answering machine came on. He left no message. North hesitated, considering the implications of calling the Belleford police. He thought about the chief who'd been complicit in a cover-up North had tried to expose when he'd worked there. North's reward? A closing of the ranks in the town, one that had almost ruined his career; the pressure had destroyed his marriage.

He made the call and got the Belleford duty desk. He identified himself, quickly summarized what had happened and asked the officer to dispatch people to Connie's parents' house. He gave the officer the address. "Proceed with caution. Some of the perpetrators may still be there."

The duty officer had a deep voice, sympathetic but also with traces of scepticism. "This call is coming from a cell phone. Is there a way for me to confirm your identity and the accuracy of this information?"

North considered a request to transfer this call to the chief or his former staff sergeant and decided against it. Instead, he left the number of the St. Thomas police and the name of Dexter Phillips. He dialled the St. Thomas station, told Dexter what had happened and said the Belleford police would be calling. Dexter said, "I've got a call on the other line. It's probably them. You're not supposed to be working. How are you going to handle that?"

"I have no idea. Go ahead and talk to them. I need time to think. Call me back and ask the Belleford police to do the same."

The call ended. North stared at the drawing of the girl with the big eyes and the round breasts without taking in any features. He rang Maddy's cell phone and was relieved when she answered right away and sounded sober. "Dad, what's going on?"

North retreated to general police language, about there being a threat. It was routine, but precautions were necessary. "Did everybody leave?"

There was excitement in Maddy's voice. "Yeah. We're like going to a hotel or something."

North said that was good, that he loved her and Dylan. He asked her to pass that along to his son. He couldn't talk any more.

"Love you, too, Dad. Be careful."

Dexter rang him to tell him he'd confirmed North's identity with the Belleford police. Somebody from that force would be calling.

CHAPTER 33

North was back in his apartment when the call came through. His first question was, "What's going on?"

"Me and my partner found the front door unlocked. The retired couple was in the kitchen. Husband and wife, bound to chairs and gagged. Chairs were duct-taped together."

North asked, "Did you say duct-taped?"

"Yes, Sir."

His heart sank. He began to sweat. "How do Howard and Betty-Anne seem?"

"He appears to have suffered a heart attack. We called the ambulance."

Connie had inherited her love of food from her father, a gentle bear of a man who was closer to 300 pounds than 200. "Did they say anything about Connie?"

"Their daughter's apparently been abducted."

"How many were involved?"

"Three men."

"Any description?"

"Not yet. Your mother-in-law's been through a lot. I'm no doctor, but she needs a sedative. She's panicking about her husband and her daughter."

"Can I talk to her?"

"I'll see what she says."

Muffled sounds, background talk. His in-laws' two-storey, yellow brick house north of downtown in Belleford would now be a crime scene. The female police officer's voice sounded in his left ear. "I'm sorry. She's in no condition to speak to anybody."

"Did she give you any information about the three men?"

"Two of them were big, middle-aged and had beards. One had a ponytail. The third one was younger. That's about all we've got."

North considered the condition Betty-Anne must be in. "See if she knows whether any of them were wearing colours. Did she say anything else about Connie?"

"We're treating this as sexual assault on top of break and enter, forcible confinement and kidnapping."

"Sexual assault?"

"Yes, Sir."

"You mean they raped Betty-Anne?"

"We are treating sexual assault as very probable."

North left the bed and kicked a chair. He dropped the telephone on the desk and punched the wall. Pain shot through his good hand. He punched it again. And again. He picked up the telephone and shouted, "What about Connie?"

"Do we have to discuss that right now?"

"I want to know. Did they rape Connie?"

"From what we've been told, it is a possibility."

North sat on the bed, raging. He blamed himself, for putting Connie at risk, for devoting more to work than to his marriage, for not insisting she stay with him after that night at the hotel. Tears came. He swiped them away.

The officer said, "Sir?"

"I'm still here." North leaned over, his left arm on his knee, the phone at his ear. He cleared his throat and straightened his back. "It's not my investigation. But based on what I'm hearing, I want Belleford Police to check every known Python or associate in the area."

"The motorcycle club?"

"No, the biker gang."

"We can't investigate people just because they ride a chopper. Bikers have their rights, too."

North said, "I'd like to say, fuck the Charter, but we need everything to stand up in court. We also can't forget an innocent older couple has been violated." He spat out the next words, "And somebody captured a woman they may have raped. All to throw me off an investigation down here."

North ended the call. There was a message waiting for him. He dialled in for it. Connie's voice. She seemed to be in pain, panting, her voice shaking. "Carl, they got me. And Mom and Dad."

## CHAPTER 34

A man snarled, his voice further from the telephone, "Tell him what to do, bitch."

Another man yelled, "Ride her hard."

Connie's voice came back, whimpering. "They want you to stop. They say they're going to..."

"You tell him, girl."

Her voice broke as she said, "I'm scared. I..."

The message ended.

North saved it and thumbed his way to messages, retrieving the incoming phone number. He called the station and asked for a check on the number. "Contact me on my cell as soon as you have anything."

It was 10:30 on Saturday night. North checked his cell phone for more messages. Nothing. He switched on the television and collapsed in a chair. The ringing of his phone startled him. Exhausted, he'd slept for a few minutes. An officer said the phone number he'd requested appeared to be a cell phone.

North closed his phone. Using his left hand, he ran his fingers through his hair. He sucked on his false tooth. He lit a cigarette and stubbed it out. He blinked his eyes and tried to think. Nothing came to him. He must be losing his mind.

He called Jennifer Duchamps at home. No answer. He didn't leave a message. He called her cell. She replied on the fifth ring. North told her he needed her help.

"I'm kind of in the middle of something."

"I'm in the middle of a lot more." North had picked up on a guarded tone in her voice, so he asked, "Are you trying to tell me something?"

"I'm with Marcel."

"As in, *with* Marcel."

"Yeah."

"Sorry, but this is huge, or I wouldn't bother you. We're real close to nailing Turk. But he got to my in-laws, and he has Connie."

"Oh, Carl, I feel for you, I really do. But... I can't... You'll have to find somebody else."

"They raped Connie."

"Oh, my God, you're sure? Of course, you are. That was stupid. I'm so sorry."

"I just got the call. I feel terrible. We were separated. Maybe that makes me feel even more guilty."

"Give me a minute."

The minute seemed to drag on forever. North paced the carpet until he heard, "Okay, I'm in the kitchen. I can't imagine...You must be..."

"I don't know what I am. But we need to stop these guys."

"I know. But, Carl..."

"What?"

"I can't."

North resumed his pacing. "Can't or won't?" He immediately hated himself, just a little, for saying this, but he did not take it back.

"Are you giving me an order? That's not your call. You're on leave."

North stopped. "I'm asking."

"I want to help, I really do. But it's Saturday night, and I'm not booked to work." Her voice became quieter, with shades of sadness. "I have to pay some attention to Marcel and this marriage. Or they'll both be gone."

"Fine." North snapped the telephone shut and threw it on the bed. The fact that she was right, that he had been in similar situations and made different choices, made him feel not one whit better.

He retrieved the phone and rang the station, asking them to contact Pete Heemstra, no matter what it took, and to have him call North on his cell.

The return call came within ten minutes. North's voice broke, once, when he was relaying what he'd learned in the last couple of hours. Only once, and it seemed to come out of nowhere. He excused himself, said he'd be back in a minute. He went to the bathroom, ran a glass of water and studied himself in the mirror. "Act like a professional" he told the worn-out-looking man with the clipped hair and the broken nose that had never been properly fixed.

He returned to his cell phone and asked Pete where he was.

"Ric's Place, shooting pool and having a couple of drinks."

"Can you get away? Come to Belleford with me?"

"Jesus, Carl, does either of us want to do that?"

"You may have a choice. I don't."

North asked him to stop by the station and bring a shotgun with him.

★

Smelling of vodka and cologne and a recent cigarette, Pete Heemstra met
North in the hotel lobby.

They wrapped the shotgun and a box of shells in a blanket in North's
trunk. North drove. Neither of them said much at first. Light snow falling
on Centennial Avenue became heavier when they hit Highbury. The wind
was from the north, the drifting serious on some of the curves. On the
large S-curve about half way to the 401, the car struck snow and rocked,
rear wheels spinning out.

"Want a hit? It'll calm your nerves."

North sipped and added one healthy belt for good measure. It burned
and warmed him and eased a tiny bit of his tension. "Thanks, Pete." He lit
a cigarette and opened the window a crack. Cold air roared around them.

The eastern run on the 401 was treacherous, new snow driving across
the four lanes, reducing visibility. North kept the heater on high and drove
at 100 kilometres per hour. Transport trucks were doing 80, their running
lights blurred by snow. Pete seemed content to nip occasionally from his
bottle and let North concentrate on his driving.

Near Woodstock, the world filled with whirling white dervishes.
North was down to 40 kilometres an hour, following the taillights of a big
truck instead of trying to figure out where the road was. He was late seeing the exit signs for the 403 to Brantford and Hamilton and careened
onto the merge lane. Within 10 kilometres, the driving on the 403 became
easier. Traffic was light. At its strongest, the wind behind the Crown
Victoria seemed to lift the suspension of the big car.

Pete said something. As if waking from a trance induced by snow driving, North turned to him. "What's that?"

"Are you ready for this?"

"You mean, Belleford?"

"Been thinking about why we left."

"I'm trying to avoid that." But even at its worst, when he had been a
long way from sure he could keep the Crown Victoria on the highway, part
of his mind had been on Belleford. A seed of insecurity, planted by the
decision to go back, was threatening to swell into full-blown anxiety.
North hated the very idea of returning. He dreaded the thought of
encountering any officers who'd served with him. His mind kept obsess-
ing about the worst side of the town, the side that had won when the
powers-that-be had buried his investigation of corruption so deep, it
would never surface again. Nobody had been prepared to accept that men

of power and influence were abusing teenage hockey players. What had saved him, or had saved enough of him that he could begin rebuilding his life, had been his transfer to St. Thomas.

He tossed the last of a cigarette out the window. "Give me another hit."

Pete passed him the bottle, but North said, "No, forget I said that."

"I got lots."

North turned away. More liquor would unnerve him, leave him addled. "So, you hate the idea of going back as much as I do?"

"Probably not." Pete shook his head. "But we have to go."

"Yeah."

"Because of Connie."

North considered his motives. "And her mom and dad. They shouldn't be mixed up in this. Plus, somebody has to stop these bastards."

Pete settled back in his seat, the bottle cradled like a baby in his left arm. "You get that way too much sometimes." He looked at North. "The more you make it personal..."

"But what's a guy supposed to do?"

"Damned if I know." Pete settled back and appeared to nod off in the warmth of the vehicle.

Forty minutes later, North braked and slid, taking the Belleford exit. The lighting at a stop sign for the road to the town was muted by falling snow. Belleford had higher drifts than St. Thomas. They passed the new subdivision where he'd found the body of a woman he'd known a little too well. Her death had set in motion an investigation of murder and, eventually, sexual abuse. North was sure he'd solved the case... what was the point of going over that ground again? North focused his attention on the road, trying to ignore the houses finished by developer Jake deBruine since North had left Belleford. Jake had won, had got North out of the way, and continued to add to his considerable fortune.

North drove as fast as he could, slowing whenever the big car slipped on icy patches, then accelerating again. The historic downtown looked wintry and well lit, even prettier than he remembered. They headed north, past newer houses encased in white vinyl, and turned east into an older neighbourhood with mixed housing.

Outside his in-laws' two-storey yellow brick home were police cars with rotating red and blue lights, yellow caution tape, investigators coming and going. North identified himself to the first officer he met and asked to speak to the Ident Officer, a woman of about 45 with dark hair, brown eyes and the calmness of a saint. So far, so good. Two officers who were focused on the case and not bringing up the past. North summarized as much as he could, including his personal relationship with the couple who owned the home and Connie, who'd apparently been abducted. Without giving the woman all the details, North brought her up-to-speed on a likely connection with the Pythons, or their associates.

"This must be horrible for you." The woman's sympathetic eyes studied North. "I can't imagine what you're going through."

Emotions roiled inside North. He looked away and said hoarsely, "Thank you."

He felt her hand on his left sleeve. "What did you do to your arm?"

"Accident in the line of duty." North glanced at his cast. "One more reason I wouldn't mind putting these guys away. What do we have from the scene?"

"Not a lot. The man and woman are at the hospital. The man's in ICU."

An officer North recognized was loading a kitchen chair into a police van. North turned away from the man's line of sight. "That's not good, not with my father-in-law's heart condition." North stamped his feet and blew into a half-closed fist he made with his left hand. "Can we talk in your car?"

It was a Crown Victoria, unmarked, very much like North's from St. Thomas. North got in the front and Pete in the back. North glanced quickly at him—Pete must have left the bottle in North's vehicle.

North updated the officer on the Pythons and Turk.

The woman said. "Bikers and mob bosses understand two things—demand absolute loyalty and make sure nothing sticks to you."

North thought about how loyal Connie had been, but refused to let his attention be distracted by that right now.

The office said, "We do know of a biker hangout north of town. Along the river."

The woman spoke into her shoulder mic and asked the dispatcher to have somebody double check on any known or suspected biker gang hangouts near Belleford. While they waited for a response, North asked how long she'd been working for the local force.

"Since October, so a few months. I transferred in when my fiancé got a job in Brantford. It's a lot quieter than Mississauga. Usually on Saturday night, we break up a domestic, arrest a drunk or two and count Timbits at the Tim Hortons. Although there's more drugs than I was expecting."

"How's Hardick?"

"I got no problems with him." She hesitated before adding, "I heard you two had issues. I can respect that."

The woman was distracted by a voice in her earpiece. She jotted down an address and said to her mic, "Ten-4, and thank you."

"You seem to have your hands full here. Constable Heemstra and I can take that, if you like." North kept his voice as calm and professional as he could manage. "I'll call if we need back-up."

The officer surveyed the scene, handed North the paper and said, "I owe you one."

★

Coming out of town, the road along the river twisted and turned. It was snow-covered to snow-packed, so North had to take it easy. A good area for bikers or their associates. Trees spiked black into the snowy night. Houses, sheds and cottages were set back from the road in groves or woodlots. About five kilometres out of town, Pete said, "Hey, you missed it. We have to turn back."

North swung into a laneway another quarter of a kilometre ahead, reversed onto the road and headed back toward the roadside number Pete had noticed. This time, he slowed before the sign. The lane was a white depression in the terrain, leading off to the right into the trees.

"Is there anything here?"

"I think I see a light." Pete lowered his window and thrust his head into the night air. "Yeah, there's somebody back there."

CHAPTER 35

The Crown Victoria slid to a stop on the edge of the road. Its interior lights glowed like the inside of a cockpit. A warm cockpit, which North hated to leave. He said to Pete, "How we going to handle this?"

"I'll stay here with my bottle," Pete murmured with a smile. "Where it's warm, and I can sleep."

"We'll call that Plan B. Plan A involves slogging through snow to whatever's up there."

"Party pooper." Pete stared out the windshield. "Let's ride straight up the lane. Sirens, lights, guns, give 'em all we got."

"Brilliant," North said. "Good way to make sure Connie's dead."

"So we go through the woods?"

"Have you ever seen a biker hideout without a dog?"

"Not that I'm any expert. But now that you mention it." Pete set the vodka bottle on the seat.

"That wind's out of the north so we'll come in from the south." North gestured ahead of the police vehicle. "That means going through the trees on that side of the road."

Pete blinked his eyes and swayed in the seat. But he sounded sober as he said, "You ready?"

"Uh-huh."

"Assuming we get past this phantom dog, what then, Sarge?"

"We work that out as we go. One step at a time."

Pete checked to make sure he had his piece in his shoulder holster. North handed him a long, black Maglite and pushed a button to unlock the trunk. The two men left the vehicle almost simultaneously. Pete was slower and called to North, asking him to wait. North told him to shut up, and when he did, North listened for sounds from the bush. All he could hear was wind rattling frozen trees and singing in hydro wires supported by skeletal towers along the river.

North retrieved the shotgun from the trunk. It was an eight-round semi-automatic Benelli, particularly useful in close-quarter situations. He checked to make sure it was fully loaded. He shoved a handful of extra shells in his left pocket. With his forearm in a cast, he wouldn't be a whole lot of use with a shotgun. He traded the weapon with Pete for the Maglite.

North said, "We're dealing with animals. If you point it at somebody, pull the trigger before you think."

Pete saluted roughly, and they set off, North ploughing a path through the snow and Pete following. The shotgun was balanced in the crook of Pete's arm, the barrel pointing down, as if he were a duck hunter.

The ditch snow was deep, up to their crotches in places. Traversing it was treacherous. North took large, dragging steps to break a path. The snow wasn't as heavy as they came out of the ditch in the never-darkness created by snow at night. He spotted the fence before they bumped into it. It took three tries before he was able to mount it, swing over and dismount. He reached over and took the gun from Pete who clambered over on the first try.

The two men zigzagged around dark tree trunks. North was circling left as they went, keeping an eye on the light glimmering ahead of them from time to time in what seemed to be an old forest. A sapling zapped him in the crotch. He was forced to stop, his breath gone. Pain surged from his groin to his abdomen. He suppressed the impulse to cry out. Pete drew up behind him and made hand signals with his gloves, asking what was wrong. Half bent over, North shook his head.

Pete swung away from him, leaned the shotgun against a tree, and fumbled with his clothing. In a minute North heard a stream of urine and inhaled its earthy fragrance. Pete zipped up. North stood.

The sharp pain was subsiding. North said very quietly, "You're leaving DNA, buddy."

"Just marking my territory."

North led off. Moving was better than staying in one place, thinking about pain.

By the time they reached the clearing, North's left foot was cold from toe to ankle from snow melting inside his boot. He paused at the edge of the trees, hunkering down, resting his cast on his right knee. He set the flashlight on a stump and felt in his left parka pocket for his piece, for reassurance. He left it there and picked up the heavy flashlight.

The house appeared to have been made of thick logs hewn from the original forest a long time ago. Smoke curled from a brick chimney. The wall they faced was solid logs, but light streamed from windows at the front and the back of the house, so the place had electricity. A barn or shed of some sort loomed over the house on the far side. There seemed to be a truck or van in front of that building. An outhouse stood among trees behind the house. The wind had picked up in the clearing. North rubbed his face and wiggled his cheek and nose muscles against creeping frostbite.

North stood. Pete touched his arm. North turned to him, and without dropping the shotgun, Pete swung both arms wide in a questioning gesture. North indicated Pete should go to the back of the house. Moving his good hand toward himself, he demonstrated that he, North, would go to the front.

They set off, North treading toe-to-heel to reduce the noise of his approach. When he reached the front corner of the house, he paused, leaning a shoulder against a rough log about 18 inches deep. Glancing to his left, he saw Pete stop at the back corner. North inhaled, held his breath, released it, and inhaled again, attempting to calm his heart rate. He turned, and, in a few short steps, was in the light from the front window. After his time in the snowy night, the light seemed as powerful as the beam from a lighthouse or a prison tower searchlight. He stepped onto a primitive porch floor constructed of thick rough planks.

The board beneath his left foot gave under him, rose at its far end and settled with a bang. To North, the sound was as loud as if Pete had pulled the trigger on the shotgun.

A dog inside woofed. A man's voice roared, "What the hell?"

A door slapped open.

A dog, so large that it temporarily blocked some of the light from the door, bounded to the porch. Apparently sensing North, it skidded on the rough boards. Veering to its right, it took two more bounds and launched itself at him.

North raised the arm in his cast. He forced it sideways, between the dog's jaws, open and eager to chow down on any part of this intruder. North felt the cast give as the jaws closed, and the head swung left and right, the animal using its weight to bring the arm down.

Raising the 30-inch Maglite in his left arm, North struck out blindly, chopping at the dog's skull. Once. Raised the light. Twice. Raised again. Three times. With the third blow, the dog crumpled and lay at his feet.

North was puffing, hauling in cold air. He leaned forward. Light showed on the porch floor as the door in front of him opened. Still half bent over, he looked up. A man in a jacket was raising an assault weapon.

Dropping the flashlight, North threw himself full length on the snow-drifted porch floor. He rolled right onto his cast, fumbling for his piece in his parka pocket. The gun snagged on material. He grunted, puffing, his heart racing from the adrenalin rush. He rolled himself left, then right as he tried to free the pistol.

Pete's shotgun blasted. The man in the doorway yelled. North glanced up as the assault weapon answered. Bullets cascaded in a wide circle, a stream of retorts going nowhere. A second roar from behind North. The assault rifle seemed to leap in the air. The man grunted and dropped to his knees.

North had his piece out. He raised and tried to steady it at the man. Behind him, Pete whispered, sounding calm. "Are you okay?"

North rolled to a sitting position. From there to his knees and back up. Through the window, he saw a kitchen with a table, chairs, a wood stove. He said as levelly and quietly as he could manage, "Anybody else in there?"

"Not sure, Sarge. I spotted one woman, possibly Connie. In a back bedroom. She's not in good shape. Didn't notice anyone else."

"Is this one dead?"

"With a shotgun, who knows? I went for a knee and an arm."

North's wind was returning. "If any of this ever gets to trial, it would be nice if you saved us a witness."

"That's what I'm thinking."

North detected movement. He raised an arm and gestured at Pete, who faded back around the side of the house. A slim man in blue jeans, suspenders drooping from his hips, torso and feet bare, entered the kitchen. One hand gripped a Saturday night special. The other, a knife. North moved right, between the window and the door.

The man in the doorway groaned. He was crawling toward the yard, as if he might escape.

The man inside called out, "Poppy, is things all right?"

The man on the porch moaned an answer but said nothing intelligible. He was off the porch, in the snow, but seemed unable to move further.

"What the fuck?" the slim man shouted. "What the fuck's goin' on?"

North considered his options. He didn't know what Pete was up to. And he didn't know whether there was also a back entrance to this building. Two possibilities. If the slim man came out the front, he'd have to come past North. If there were two doors, Pete likely had him at the back.

North waited.

Branches clicked in the wind. Snow stung his cheeks. Without letting go of his piece he rubbed his face with his fingers and blew on those fingers to warm them. He wanted to stamp his feet—to assure himself he still had full circulation in them—but he didn't dare.

Noises and muffled bumps came from inside the kitchen. A man swore.

The front door creaked as it opened, slowly.

In the semi-darkness between the door and the window, North had a night-vision advantage. Before the man stepped outside, North dropped to one knee.

The man had on a parka—flopping open—boots and no hat. He looked wildly in every direction. He glanced at the downed man, who tried to say something. The slim man kept moving, away from North, stumbling along the porch boards, his boots loose and scraping on snow. Keys clinked.

The man reached the far corner of the porch. He took the first step down.

As if materializing out of nowhere, Pete stepped around the corner of the house. A flurry of motion. No shots. The man grunted and doubled over. More movements. The man's head snapped back. He dropped to a drift on the bottom step. Pete seemed to fall with him.

North jumped off the porch and ran toward them. By the time he reached Pete, the officer had a knee in the man's back and was handcuffing his wrists behind him.

"Nice play, Shakespeare," North said.

Pete looked up at him and said, "He's not going anywhere. We need to check the house."

CHAPTER 36

The kitchen ceiling was low. Its logs were blackened in one area, where a stovepipe went up through a metal sleeve. The floor was bare pine boards, unswept, sticky underfoot. Logos from Jack Daniels cases had been stapled four feet high on one wall. Half a bottle of Jack Daniels sat on the table beside three glasses and a soup bowl overflowing with the butts of cigarette and roaches.

Pete ducked as he followed North out of the kitchen, through a doorway leading to a short hall with two rooms off it. "She's in the one on the left," Pete told North.

As he entered the room, he felt as if he'd been zapped in the groin for the second time in one night. For a moment, he couldn't breathe.

What was it with these sickos and duct tape?

Connie seemed to be topsy-turvy, her head at the foot of the bed. Her mouth was taped shut. Her arms were behind her back. She had on a man's leather jacket. One leg was taped to a dark wooden headboard.

The room was illuminated by a single bulb in an overhead socket. It was cool in the room. The two sources of heat seemed to be from the kitchen, through the door, and from a squat electric heater in the corner.

A stand by the bed had a routered, now splintered, design at its top. A Jack Daniels bottle and two lines of cocaine were on the stand.

The blanket under Connie was the colour of faded mustard. There were brown stains on it, from her blood. More blood had dried brown around her upper legs. Redder liquid continued to seep. She was naked from the waist down. Shivering.

A sleeping bag had been tossed on the floor. North forced himself to take four steps into the room, grab the blanket and spread it over Connie's lower body.

"It's okay," he said, although nothing here seemed remotely close to okay.

Pete was near North. He leaned the shotgun between the wall and the nightstand. He half-whispered to North, "Anything I can do?"

North raised the arm in the cast and said, in a voice as steady as he could muster, a tone he kept dead calm despite the shock and rage he was feeling. "I could use a little help to free her."

North touched Connie's cheek. She flinched, flung her head away from him. Her eyes widened and scrunched shut. North removed his hand and said, "It's me, Connie. It's Carl, your husband." Even as he uttered those last two words, he wondered whether he would live to regret them.

But he did not hesitate. He said, as calmly and as steadily as before, "It's me, Carl. Can you hear me?"

Her head turned fractionally back toward him. North reached over and brushed strands of hair off her forehead. "Good, you can hear me. We're going to help you. This is Pete Heemstra, you remember him from the Belleford Police."

"Hi, Connie. Sorry to have to see you this way. This is going to hurt, just for a minute. I'll do it fast." Pete's fingers picked at grey tape around her ankle and yanked at an end he found. In short jerks that tore the tape about three inches at a time, he released her foot in less than a minute. He moved the foot to the mattress. Her lower leg vibrated.

"Con, you're going to feel this, but I'll do it quick, okay? Here I go." North grabbed the duct tape near her mouth, hesitated for a second and then ripped it, two strips in one motion.

Connie cried out and squirmed, her eyes tearing again. North stroked her hair, her cheek. "Sorry, Con, sorry I had to do that. But it's over. Can you help us? Roll a little to the right, okay? That's it. Just one more thing we gotta do." And to Pete, he said, "Help me out."

It took longer to free her wrists than her leg. Pete worked at the tape feverishly before pulling out his pocket knife and slicing it, from her skin outward, splitting the tape so he could peel it back.

With North's help, Connie shifted her hands in front of her. She rubbed her wrists and slid her hands under the sleeping bag. She closed her eyes, rolled away from the men and curled into the foetal position, wrists between her legs.

She said nothing.

North reached over and touched her shoulder. Her body quivered. The shoulder jerked away. He said, "It's me, Con. It's Carl. It's all right. We have everything under control. Pete's going to leave now. He's going to make sure the other men are secure."

North switched his attention to Pete and said, "I want both men in the kitchen. And don't call the station just yet."

"What about..." Pete nodded toward Connie.

"Ten minutes isn't going to make any difference. We got one shot at this. Maybe."

Pete left. North said to Connie, his voice soft and comforting. "We're going to get you some help."

Later, North wouldn't be able to recall his words. He kept talking, in something of a trance, offering words of assurance. He didn't care whether or not he repeated himself. He tried to reach her, once, by touching her again, but she shrank away from him.

Pete stuck his head in and said, "One guy, sorry. He didn't make it. I tried to revive him, but he lost too much blood."

"What about the other guy?"

"Groggy but awake."

"Thanks."

"It's the skinny guy. He's in the kitchen, handcuffed to the table and the doorknob. Claims to have a terrible headache."

"I'll be out in a minute."

"The dog came around. Pretty passive, but I tied him up outside."

After Pete left, North shifted so he could lie on the bed beside Connie. He curled an arm around her, and she left it there. Connie kept her face away from him. Her shivering seemed to be lessening.

"I have to go for a bit, Connie. I'll be right back. I promise." He went to the adjoining bedroom and found a second sleeping bag to cover Connie.

"Thanks," she burbled in a voice that was little more than a whisper.

North settled on the mattress and leaned over. He didn't try to touch her skin. Instead, he ran his fingers through her hair, gently over and over. After a while he said, "There's something I have to do, Con."

She whispered words he couldn't catch. He leaned closer, and heard her say, "Get me out of here."

Her involuntary shaking started up again. North wanted to pull her to himself, but he didn't think she was ready. He said, "Soon, Con, real soon. I have to do a few things, and then we'll get you out of here."

It felt cruel, as if he were abandoning her, but North left.

★

The man in the kitchen had a magenta bruise under his chin from the butt end of Pete's shotgun. The discolouration looked as if it would spread over the next few hours, up to his gaunt cheeks and down to his scrawny neck. His arms, spread wide, were cuffed at the wrist to the table and the door.

"Release him from that end," North gestured toward the door.

Once Pete had done that, North pulled a chair close to the man, his face less than two feet away. The man hadn't shaved in a day or two. His hair was cropped short, and white scalp showed through it. He had a narrow nose and his lips formed a thin line. North looked directly into his frightened brown eyes, "I have more hate for you than any man I've ever met." This wasn't the strict truth. The man was such a pathetic loser, it would be impossible to hate him for long. "You know why you're on the receiving end of all this hate?"

With his left hand, North pulled a duMaurier package out of his shirt pocket. He lit one and blew smoke in the pathetic loser's face. "I didn't hear you."

The man shook his head. His eyes veered toward Pete, who stood behind North, and back to stare down at North's feet.

"Look at me, you miserable... Where I come from, men don't rape women."

The man's eyes rose to North's chest.

"Higher. I want you to look me square in the face. There, that's better. Now, don't look away. 'Cause when I turn back, I want to see your eyes right on me."

North swivelled in his chair and asked Pete, "If you call the Belleford station, how long will it take for emergency services to get here?"

"A night like this, 10 minutes or so, if they don't get lost."

"I want you to call them. Remember the number?"

"Oh, yeah."

North turned back, and the man's eyes were fully on his. "You have 10 minutes to make up your mind."

The man started to say something. He couldn't get it out the first time. He tried again. "About what?"

"About whether you want to testify against Turk and enter witness protection. Or do life without parole for kidnapping and raping my wife." The man's eyes widened. "If you like neither alternative, me and Pete can drag you outside near your buddy, and Pete can put a bullet through your skull. I don't see how anybody would complain about that, do you, Pete?"

"Nobody I can think of, right off hand."

The man's eyes darted around and came back. "That's illegal."

"You're wasting my time. Pete's call is going through, and the clock is ticking."

The man swallowed and said nothing. He asked for a cigarette, and North said he couldn't think of a good reason to do the man any favours. Not one.

When Pete finished his telephone call, North looked at his watch. "Eight and a half minutes. Doesn't time go fast when we're having fun?"

"What if I don't know any Turk?"

"Then you know nothing about a million dollars' worth of cocaine in that boogey van outside. And you're absolutely no good to us as a witness. So what does that leave us, Pete?"

"I take him outside for some personal target practice."

North said, "Your DNA is going to be all over the woman in the bedroom, you and that other guy, the one who passed away tonight. Am I wrong about that?"

The man swallowed and asked again for a cigarette.

Pete said, "Might help him think, Sarge." He shook out a cigarette from North's package, lit it in his own mouth and passed it to the thin man's lips. They eagerly glommed onto the filter.

The man inhaled, blew smoke out through his nostrils, coughed gently and said, "How good is witness protection?"

North knew he had him. He didn't hurry. He took a deep drag on his own cigarette and said, "If we can protect mobsters, a few guys on Harleys shouldn't be a problem."

"If I go up against Turk, I walk away from the rape and the kidnap?"

"We have to get Turk on more than the drug charges," North said. "Did he order this thing tonight?"

The man nodded. "He was with us, in Belleford, when we picked her up."

That gave North pause. "A Scenes of Crime office said there were three of you. I assume you know about the murders in the St. Thomas area? The death at the strip club and the farmer, Hughie Campbell? The attempt on Candy's life? Are you high enough in the organization to testify about them?"

"What organization?" The man snorted as he exhaled a stream of smoke. "In this area, it was just Turk and a few guys. I know enough to put that man away forever."

"So you will testify against him?"

"Long as you look after me."

"One thing, maybe you can clear up for me. We heard the van wasn't coming until tomorrow."

The man's mouth twitched. "With the weather, we sent it early. Then got waylaid with this other deal." He almost smiled, but North's look ended that inclination.

CHAPTER 37

North was in the kitchen of the log house when a woman from the OPP sexual assault unit left the bedroom and stopped by to see him. She sipped from a cardboard container of coffee that must have been cold and said, "She asked to see you."

"Did you get anything from her?"

The woman had short, curly hair and a maternal demeanour. She shook her head. "It's too soon. We'll get a statement at the hospital."

"How about samples?"

The woman offered a tired smile. "No problem."

"And DNA from the dead man and the suspect?"

"Oh, yeah."

"That skinny dude. We need to get him some place safe tonight."

The woman swallowed the last of her coffee. "Between us and the RCMP, we're pretty good at that."

"So I can leave him with you?"

"That's the best thing."

"What should I say to Connie?"

"Keep it fairly neutral." The woman placed a hand on his shoulder. "Anything that will help her see it's not her fault."

"First, I need to call St. Thomas."

He reached the station, and gave the duty officer a detailed account of what had happened. "We have to pick up Turk, and we have to do it tonight. He's probably at the farm, but he could be staying at the Amber Lee or the Church Street apartment in town. Get on it now. If he has the slightest hint we're after him, he'll be gone."

"Yes, Sir."

"I want everybody on this, from both forces. Now repeat everything I just told you. There can be no errors on this one, and overtime will not be an issue."

When he was satisfied, he ended that conversation and called Jennifer. Her cell phone was off, so he tried her at home. The answering machine came on. He called back four times before she picked up. He told her about his night and asked her to go to the station, to make sure everybody had their heads screwed on right.

Jennifer said she would. "I'm sorry. I hate it that I couldn't help you earlier."

"I wanted to apologize for losing it. You made the right call."

"How's your wife?"

"I'll tell you about that later."

"Okay, Carl. Take it slow. She needs you right now."

"I know. Thanks. I've got my cell on, and we'll be back as soon as we can. I'd love to be there when we bring this guy in."

"I'll call you."

★

Connie huddled by the bed on a kitchen chair. She was wearing a sweater and slacks. She had a sleeping bag over her shoulders. The electric heater was on high, the room becoming hot.

North sat on the bed near her. The other sleeping bag was covering the stains. He removed a clear plastic glove from his good hand.

As he did this, Connie looked at the cast on his forearm, avoiding his eyes. Her voice was low and harsh. "Neither one of us looks too good, sweets."

North fixed his gaze on the floor. "We'll get through this."

"I shouldn't have let them in." Tears followed behind those words. "I should have..."

"Don't say that; don't even think it. None of this is your fault." North thought about how much was his responsibility. "We got here as soon as we could."

"How are Mom and Dad?"

"I think they're going to be okay." He avoided the topic of her father and his heart.

"Will you go with me, to the hospital?"

"I can't. I have to follow..." North's gaze shifted up, to eyes staring at him, as if she were still in shock. He thought about all the times he'd said things like that to her, and where that approach had got him. "Yeah, I'm going with you."

Her eyes were filling, her round cheeks scrunching her eyes into slits.

★

North rode in the back of the ambulance with Connie. They were in Emergency at Brantford General when North's cell phone vibrated in his pocket against his chest. He glanced at the number—Jennifer's cell.

"We got Turk."

"What does that mean, exactly?" North was off his chair, pacing away from Connie. There must have been a dozen people sitting or lying around the perimeter of the room.

"He's in custody. We're holding him in St. Thomas."

North had to refrain from punching the air with a fist and hollering, "Yes." He took two steps and said, "Where was he?"

"Sound asleep at the Amber Lee. One woman with him and a couple of other guys down the hall. Nothing to it, this time. Guess nobody got to him in advance."

North took his time walking back to Connie. He stood in front of her chair and told her Turk had been arrested. She rocked on her chair. Chewing on her bottom lip. Moaning as if she couldn't stop. North moved over to sit beside her. He put an arm around. Her head shifted. Her cheek was warm against his shoulder. Gradually, over a few minutes, the rocking motion ceased.

## EPILOGUE

North wondered, were those tights Maddy was wearing, or were they jeans? And that man who'd given his 15-year-old daughter the once-over when she and Dylan had entered the Golden Griddle in Burlington, was he 25 or 30? But North didn't say anything. He should be grateful—if she had tattoos or piercings, they were camouflaged by her loose pink sweater.

Standing up, as if meeting her for a first date, he said, "Hi. You look nice."

"Thanks, Dad. You, too."

Dylan had a stud through his lower lip. His hair, his jacket, his slim jeans and his Doc Martens were all dark. As was his tone of voice as he said, "Hi," and swung smoothly out of the way so North couldn't muss his hair, as he used to when Dylan was 10.

Maddy ordered Belgian waffles, triple berry with whipped cream, and a Coke on the side. To keep her company, North ordered Belgian waffles with apple and added bacon and a coffee. Dylan ordered coffee. His pale face was dotted with pimples. He slouched in his chair and made drumming noises on the table with his index fingers, until North wanted to slap him. But he didn't. Instead, he asked how the music thing was going.

"Good," Dylan's voice was cracking.

"And how's school going?"

"Good."

He could not ask any of the other things that came to mind. Are you in a punk band? Doing drugs? Having sex? Any interest in growing up? Acting like a man?

It was a relief when Maddy said, "We're both okay, Dad. How are you? I mean, since what happened and everything."

A line from Johnny Cash's *American Recordings* came to mind: *I'm like a soldier getting over the war.* He said, "Better than a week ago. It takes a while."

"I saw you on the news."

Dylan chortled, a sound close to a laugh, and North glanced at him. "Did you see it?"

Dylan shrugged and slurped from his cup. "Have you like seen the serving chick?"

"You want something?"

"More coffee."

North signalled Courtney, their wait-staff.

Maddy smiled, her lips as pink as her sweater. Lipstick was her only make-up. That was also a relief. She said, "What happened to that woman from Europe or wherever. Would we have seen her when we visited?"

"No."

"Was she like helping you?"

"You could say she was undercover. I visited her at the hospital a couple of days ago. She's much better."

Their waffles arrived. North saw the size of his order and announced the start of his exercise program next week.

Maddy deliberately took small forkfuls and wiped her mouth with a napkin after each one. "How's your arm?"

North held up his cast. "Not bad. I get this thing off next week."

"How'd it happen?"

"Accident in the line of duty. No big deal."

Dylan released an embarrassing laugh again. This time, North ignored him.

Maddy said, "Connie called me."

North stopped eating and set his fork on the table. He picked up his coffee mug and blew across the top. It was noisy in the restaurant. Noisy and crowded and hot.

A baby began to cry. Irritated, North shot a look at it. A slim woman picked it up and rocked it, trying to get it to take a soother. Shut up, North thought. He was sweating. He should excuse himself and go for a cigarette. Instead, he asked, "What did you guys talk about?"

"School and stuff. It was lame, but I didn't know what to say."

North stood up, removed his jacket and hung it over the back of his chair. "I feel the same sometimes. But I see her every day. They gave me a couple of weeks off, and I drive to Brantford. We go for coffee or a walk. Or watch TV, whatever she feels like doing." He was cooling off. The baby's crying seemed to be diminishing. He took a sip of coffee.

"Is she going to like testify."

"Probably."

"I'd hate that."

"I'm doing what I can to help her."

"So, are you two like not separated?"

"Yeah," North said, "We're like not separated."

Courtney came with coffee. Dylan added cream and sugar to his and announced he was starving. Could he have steak and eggs, and if he got drums, would North pay for half?

North reached with his good hand but stopped himself from ruffling his son's hair. He looked out through wide windows. Snow was adhering to snow and falling in huge white chunks, everything sticking to everything else.

## ACKNOWLEDGEMENTS

This is a work of fiction and entirely my responsibility, but I am most grateful for the assistance of many people, including my first and best reader Nancy Kelly Carroll, and Beverley Daurio, who sees and understands so much about writing and stories. I would like to gratefully acknowledge the assistance of retired St. Thomas Police Constable Glenn Hodgson for his help in the early stages of the novel, and St. Thomas Fire Department Chief Fire Prevention Officer Bill Todd for his technical expertise. Readers Liz, Angie and Josie Carroll, Donna Mason, Margaret Sharzer and Brent Spilak all provided valuable insights. And the last should be first—sincere appreciation to the entire monthly writers' group, The Vicious Circle, consisting of Donna Mason and Richard Harding, Lion and Margaret Sharzer and Nancy Kelly Carroll.

Also, sincere appreciation to the people of St. Thomas and Elgin County, who support creative activities in many, many ways. Here and there, I have taken certain liberties with the geography of the city and the county. For this, I hope I may, in the long run, be forgiven.

— *Terry Carroll*